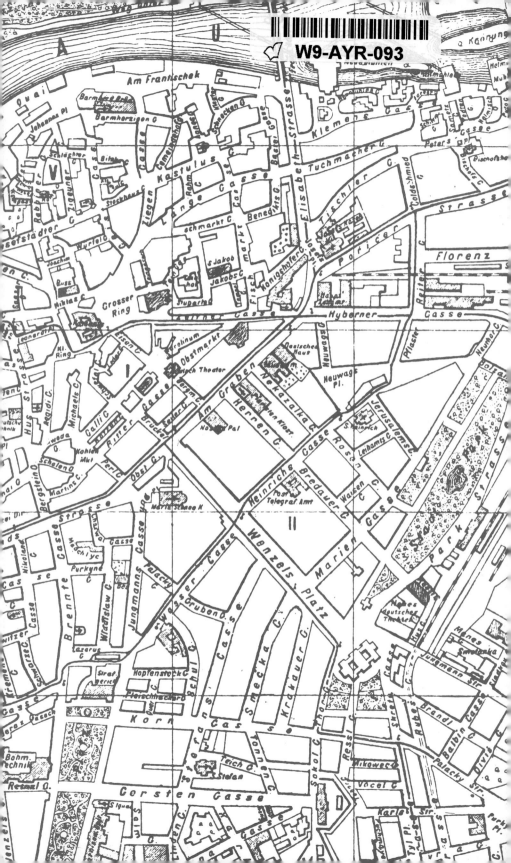

Paul Matthews
Princeton, NJ
2000

Two
Stories of
Prague

Two
Stories of
Prague

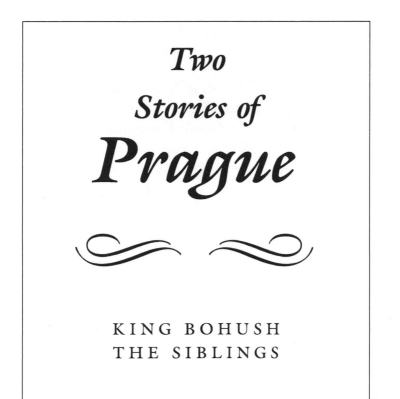

KING BOHUSH
THE SIBLINGS

by

Rainer Maria Rilke

Introduced and translated by
Angela Esterhammer

University Press of New England
Hanover and London

University Press of New England,
Hanover, NH 03755

ACKNOWLEDGMENTS

MY WORK ON RILKE'S early prose has been an ongoing occupation for several years, alongside other projects, and a number of individuals and institutions have provided generous support during that time. I would like to thank the Department of Germanic Languages and Literatures of Princeton University and the Vice President's Special Research Fund of the University of Western Ontario for grants that allowed me to do research in Prague and at the Deutsches Literaturarchiv, Marbach, Germany. I am also grateful to Ralph Freedman for first suggesting the project to me; to Marcela Moc for research assistance and her translations from Czech; to Joachim W. Storck and Alois Hofman for friendly receptions in Marbach and Prague, respectively; and to Thomas L. McFarland of the University Press of New England for enthusiastically supporting the project and garnering useful advice from readers of the manuscript. Finally, my colleagues in the Department of Modern Languages and Literatures, University of Western Ontario, as well as my parents, deserve thanks for assorted helpful suggestions.

Angela Esterhammer
London, Canada
September 1993

A NOTE ON THE
TRANSLATION

BESIDES THE CHALLENGES posed by Rilke's fluid and lyrical prose style, which many translators have commented on, his practice with regard to Czech names in *Two Stories of Prague* presents a particular problem of translation. My two guiding principles, in order of importance, have been to give an accurate impression of when Rilke uses Czech names and when he uses German ones, and to provide enough information to allow readers to identify the places mentioned in the stories on a map of Prague. Therefore, I have tried to use English transliterations of Czech wherever Rilke used German transliterations (*čaj* = "German" *Tschaj* = "English" *czay*), and to translate the word or name entirely into English when Rilke translated it into German (Czech Mostecká = Brückengasse = Bridge Street). In the case of some of the most important place-names in the text, this means that (for instance) Malá Strana has become Lesser Town because Rilke used the German Kleinseite, but Hradčany remains Hradčany in the English text to reflect the fact that Rilke used the "Germanized" pronunciation Hradschin. It should be kept in mind that Rilke's German place-names were actually in use by Prague Germans, whereas the English translations remain artificial equivalents (though they can sometimes be found today on translated city maps and in tourist information).

The topography of Prague is represented very accurately in the stories, and following it adds to an appreciation for Rilke's sense of the city and its character. Especially when dealing with place-names, therefore, I have tried to provide modern Czech equivalents and further information in the footnotes to the text.

The text of *Zwei Prager Geschichten* I have used is found in the standard edition of Rilke's *Sämtliche Werke,* 6 volumes, edited by Ernst Zinn in association with the Rilke-Archiv and Ruth Sieber-Rilke (Frankfurt a.M.: Insel, 1955–1966). In the following introduction I have quoted Rilke's other works from published translations whenever possible; otherwise, all translations of German material are my own.

INTRODUCTION

RAINER MARIA RILKE IS BEST KNOWN to English-speaking readers as a magnificent poet of the early twentieth century. From the volumes that founded his international reputation, including the *Book of Pictures* (1902, 1906), the *Book of Hours* (1905), and *New Poems* (1907–1908), to the remarkable *Duino Elegies* (1923) and *Sonnets to Orpheus* (1923), the texts of his maturity have been published countless times in English translations. While the poetry is considered his masterwork, Rilke is also much loved as a writer of lyrical prose, as in the prose poem *The Lay of the Love and Death of Cornet Christoph Rilke* (1906), the novel *The Notebooks of Malte Laurids Brigge* (1910), and his abundant correspondence with poets and artists, lovers and friends.

All these are the works of a man who, with remarkable determination, molded himself into a cosmopolitan writer, sustained intimate relationships with artists and aristocrats, and cultivated a myth of almost mystical inspiration around the creation of his most famous poems. The person Rilke was before this effective process of self-fashioning began is much less well known, especially to English readers. Rilke was born in Prague in 1875, and the story of his childhood and adolescence is a story of domestic, social, and political tensions in a city imbued with a consciousness of religion, superstition, and grand but often tragic history. Photographs of Rilke in his early twenties reveal him to be a thick-lipped, heavy-lidded young man with an expression that is either severe or else strangely unfocused. As the product of a broken home and a haphazard education, he struggled to come to terms with the influence of a difficult and demanding mother and a father who was considered a professional failure. Determined to be a writer, Rilke was thwarted in that ambition by the unpropitious cultural conditions in his native city. He was so different from the mature poet we are acquainted with that he even bore a different name. The process by which René Rilke rebaptized himself Rainer, fled from provincial Prague to the literary capitals of Europe, and concluded a pact with his past is the process recorded in two novellas he produced while in his early twenties: the *Zwei Prager Geschichten*, or *Two Stories of Prague*.

Once Rainer Rilke had established his reputation as a cosmopolitan writer, he developed an aversion to inquiries into his childhood, youth, and early career, and to the reprinting of his earliest texts. To cite one famous example, in 1921 Rilke wrote to Robert Heinz Heygrodt to stress "how strongly I resist and oppose all dragging forth and explaining of my so-called 'early period.'"[1] "Those unfortunately extant experiments cannot really be made use of *for anything*," Rilke continued, "they are not, in any, any way the beginning of my work, far rather the most private end of my childish and youthful helplessness." But Rilke does not specify at what point the youthful helplessness turns into the beginning of his mature achievement, and there are many reasons for regarding *Two Stories of Prague* as the crucial stage in his development of a polished prose style. Better than any other piece of Rilke's work, these stories reveal his evolution into an adult, a successful writer, and a different person. Rilke brought these changes about by a process of working at and achieving the fruition of his own past, which necessarily involved rejecting and distancing himself from many elements of it. The city of Prague figures in Rilke's evolution not only as the past that is both comprehended and denied, but also as a parallel model for growth and evolution, since Rilke habitually portrays the Czech people as an immature race gradually emerging into complete adulthood as a nation.

René Rilke in Prague

Though three biographies of Rilke have appeared in English during the past decade, most of the books and articles dealing specifically with Rilke's upbringing in and relationship to Prague have not been translated from the original German or Czech.[2] Two biographical and critical works focusing on Rilke's early years have had an especially powerful influence on Rilke scholarship. *René Rilke* was written in 1932 by Carl Sieber, who was married to Rilke's daughter yet never met the poet himself, and Peter Demetz's *René Rilkes Prager Jahre* (*René Rilke's Prague Years*) appeared in 1953.[3] Sieber's work, based mainly on family documents and interviews, has been contested on many points by Demetz and others who reinterpret Rilke's development more objectively in the context of historical circumstances.

Among the factors stressed by all biographers is the socially unequal marriage of Rilke's parents, which caused his well-born mother to become increasingly frustrated by her alliance with a failed army officer who finally took a position as a railway official. Sophia Rilke's dissatisfaction with her husband, combined with her excessive grief over the baby daughter she had lost a year before her second child, René, was born and the narrow-minded attitudes that she shared with most late-nineteenth century Prague Germans, contributed to the upheavals in Rilke's upbringing and education. Biographers debate the extent to which Rilke was affected psychologically and artistically by some of the more disruptive aspects of his early life, including the facts that his mother dressed and treated him like a girl until he was ready for school at age seven, and that he was then sent in rapid succession to a military college, a business school, and a series of private tutors. Between his father's lack of support and respect for Rilke's chosen career and his mother's increasing arrogance about her son's status as an up-and-coming writer, Rilke's domestic situation was hardly conducive to his artistic development.

Introduction

Rilke's mother, Sophia (or Phia), had literary ambitions herself, and her single volume of aphorisms appeared in December 1899, just after her son had published *Two Stories of Prague*. Rilke's perspective on his domestic situation during this period may be inferred from the *Two Stories of Prague*, which reflect his strong, almost superstitious feelings about motherhood, but also his criticism of stiff Prague German attitudes and, to a lesser extent, his ambivalence about formal education and about the life-style of artists and intellectuals. While the majority of critics have passed over the Prague stories as insignificant to Rilke's career, several have nevertheless noted the apparent caricature of Rilke's parents in the characters of Colonel and Mrs. Meering von Meerhelm in "The Siblings." Peter Demetz finds an allusion to Rilke's father's failed military career in the story of the old Colonel who is so often passed over for promotion that he ends up in an impotent early retirement, and who tries to make up for his professional failure by fancying himself an elegant and charming ladies' man.[4] The proud, formal, domineering, and very German Mrs. Meering von Meerhelm reminds Rilke's biographer Wolfgang Leppmann of Rilke's mother.[5]

Yet Rilke's familial situation is most clearly delineated in another story he wrote during the late 1890s, "Ewald Tragy," and the biographical experiences that enter most directly into *Two Stories of Prague* have more to do with his social and cultural interaction with his native city. The stories reflect Rilke's intense involvement in the literary and artistic circles of both Germans and Czechs in 1890s Prague. While living with his aunt in Prague's New Town and studying with private tutors, and especially after receiving a belated high school diploma in 1895, Rilke was involved in a frenzied quest to establish a literary career. He joined literary and artistic societies, contributed to newspapers and journals, edited the regional edition of a Strasbourg journal, and participated to the fullest in the coffeehouse artists' life-style that he parodies in "King Bohush." By September of 1896, however, Rilke felt it necessary to break with

Prague. He relocated to Munich, where he sporadically attended seminars in philosophy and aesthetics at the university while continuing his determined attempt to gain recognition as a writer. In the following years he moved several times between various cities, including Munich, Venice, Florence, Wolfratshausen, and Berlin, generally in the company of his newfound friend and lover, Lou Andreas-Salomé. By the end of 1898 René Rilke was living near Lou's Berlin residence in the rural suburb of Schmargendorf. It was in these surroundings and from this relative distance that he looked back on Prague and his adolescence to write "King Bohush" and "The Siblings," stories that were begun in late 1897 and first published in Stuttgart in 1899 by Adolf Bonz. While they have never before appeared in English, a Czech translation by Jan Lowenbach was published in 1908 by J. Otto, and a French translation by Maurice Betz appeared in Paris during the 1930s, published by Émile-Paul; "Le Roi Bohusch" was published in 1931, and both stories together, under the title *Contes de Bohême,* in 1939.

Prague in the 1890s

For all that the Prague stories reveal about Rilke's personal development, their more explicit subject, as the title of the volume suggests, is the city of Prague itself. Some familiarity with the city's history and its conditions in the 1890s is indispensable to an appreciation of the novellas. At the end of the nineteenth century, the city had about 350,000 inhabitants, one-tenth of whom were German and most of the rest Czech. Almost half of the German-speaking residents were Jewish; the rest of the Germans, and the Czechs, were mainly Catholic. The inner city of Prague, where Rilke's stories take place, had a higher concentration of German residents than the suburbs, where Germans were vastly outnumbered. But the most significant aspect of social life in Prague during that era was the unequal and artificial distribution of the two groups, German and Czech, in the economic structure of the city and the surrounding province, Bohemia. The majority of German inhabitants belonged to the commercial and professional establishment in Prague; they owned a disproportionate amount of property and managed many of the factories. Since Prague was part of the Austro-Hungarian empire, the military presence maintained by the Austrian government also contributed to the dominance of the German-speaking population. By contrast, service industry employees, domestic servants, and factory workers were almost uniformly Czech. Czech servants were so ubiquitous in both German and Czech households that they became stock characters in Prague German fiction. To this class belongs Mrs. Wanka's servant Rosalka in "The Siblings" and even Mrs. Wanka herself, in her role as occasional seamstress in the Meering von Meerhelm household.

The tension and antagonism between Germans and Czechs that Rilke depicts at the end of "King Bohush" is a fair representation of the ethnic climate of Prague in the 1890s. The German minority was becoming increasingly reactionary and repressive as it felt its security threatened by a growing Czech independence movement, as well as by the inroads that Czechs were making in the middle class and in civil service, by Czech dominance in local government, and by the general rate of increase of the Czech population. The great majority of Germans preferred to maintain a strict cultural isolation from the Czechs, an attitude aptly illustrated by Rilke's parents, who refused to allow their son to attend the optional Czech language classes offered by his school. Strictly observed conventions discouraged any German from attending the Czech theater, or German critics from taking note of its performances, and no Czech word or name appeared in the German papers without an accompanying German translation. As the historian Gary Cohen writes, "The self-image of the middle-class Germans as members of a cultured elite with a special unifying mission in Austria certainly distinguished them from their Czech neighbours."[6] While the Germans were motivated by their shrinking numbers and the perceived threat to their culture, the desire for segregation prevailed on the side of the Czechs as well, and the two ethnic groups increasingly maintained separate social and cultural institutions.

The separation of the cultures is reflected in many of the details of Rilke's Prague stories, from the opening sentence of "King Bohush," which refers to "Prague's *Czech* theater," to the dramatically different accounts of the action reported by Czech and German newspapers at the end of the story. In "The Siblings," the door slamming and feigned incomprehension that Ernst Land encounters when he inquires in German about a room to let in a Czech neighborhood, and his eventual resort to a stumbling *Kuchel-Böhmisch* or Pidgin Czech, is another realistic illustration of the linguistic barrier. Linguistic issues, in fact, formed the focal point of the ethnic struggle in Bohemia during the 1890s. In 1891, the municipal government in Prague voted to remove German street signs and advertising to emphasize the Czech character of the Bohemian capital. The Czechs increasingly won concessions on the language front, such as the right to use their own language alongside German in the lower courts, while the German-speaking population grew increasingly anxious and annoyed at these reforms.

What makes the account of Rilke's experience in Prague so intriguing is that he himself defied many of the conventions and became more thoroughly involved in the Czech cultural scene than would be expected, or even respectable, for a German-speaking resident. This is clear both from the *Two Stories of Prague* themselves and from external evidence, although the details of Rilke's activities in the year or so before he left Prague are obscured by his later reluctance to talk about aspects of his early career, a reluctance that sometimes caused him to misremember or falsify aspects of his experience during this period. It is even difficult to be certain whether or not Rilke spoke Czech. As the Czech scholar Václav Černý has observed, critics' opinions on the matter seem to vary depending on their own cultural allegiance: "His German biographers don't believe in his knowledge of Czech, the Czech ones like to overestimate it."[7] Many German writers seem to have accepted without question Carl Sieber's claim that Rilke didn't know a word of Czech. When the Czech Rilke scholar Clara Mágr investigated this claim, however, she discovered compelling testimony to the fact that Rilke spoke Czech quite comprehensibly, if not perfectly.[8] Mágr reports that the writer Jiří Karásek de Lvovic, one of the few Prague acquaintances of Rilke's to survive past the Second World War, claimed that Rilke preferred to speak to his Czech literary acquaintances in their own language, even though they were all fluent in German. There is also evidence that Rilke not only read but kept up a correspondence with the leading Czech literary journal *Moderní Revue*, which published poems of his both in German and in Czech translation. Rilke's involvement with Czech writers, his reading of contemporary Czech poetry (apparently in the original), and his appreciation of Czech theater stands in sharp contrast to the behavior of most writers of the time, who boycotted the activities of the rival cultural group.

Rilke's Prague stories demonstrate his reaction against the narrow-minded insularity of Prague German culture. He violates convention when he scatters throughout the Prague stories selected words and names, such as *"Tschaj"* for Czech *čaj* (tea) and *"Tschas"* for *Čas* (time; here, the *Times*), transliterating them phonetically into German without actually translating them. It may be that he has taken this habit so far as to seem to be an affectation, a contrived way of adding local color and an air of authenticity to these tales of Prague's Czech community. But in the context of the severe prejudice and segregation maintained by his society, in which cultural tension often centered on language issues, one should be aware that there is also an aspect of defiance in this practice. It is likely that Rilke's portrayal of Germans as caricatures, in contrast to his often noble and sympathetic Czech characters, would have caused a scandal in his Prague German community if he had been a better known writer at the time.

Rilke's unflattering portraits of Prague German society in

Introduction

Two Stories of Prague are confirmed by other stories he wrote in the late 1890s, such as "Ewald Tragy" and "The Family Dinner." In view of his bitter criticism of his own cultural group in these early writings, some critics have argued that the harsh pronouncements Rilke later made about his background, and his disinclination to return to his native city, are less a rejection of Prague in general than a rejection of the isolation, abstraction, and artificiality of Prague German culture in particular. In fact, after Czechoslovakia gained independence from the Austrian empire in 1918, Rilke made a point of obtaining a Czech passport and openly declared his Czech citizenship as well as his support for President Masaryk and the new regime. Investigating this development in Rilke's attitude toward the Czech nation, Joachim Storck discovers abundant evidence for Rilke's benevolent interest in Czech activities in the last years of his life, ranging from his subscription to a Prague newspaper to his acknowledgment of Czechoslovakia as his homeland and of Czechoslovakian acquaintances as compatriots.[9]

Similarly, Rio Preisner has argued that Rilke's youthful interest in Czech nationalism, history, and legend, reflected above all in *Two Stories of Prague,* represents a rejection of Prague German attitudes and an attempt to replace them with a more congenial way of relating to his homeland.[10] According to Peter Demetz, some Prague German literature in the 1890s was beginning to embrace Slavic history and the Czech linguistic heritage as a defense against the poverty of the Prague German language, a dialect cut off from the centers of literary and linguistic development. An essay Rilke wrote in 1900 supports this idea. As in *Two Stories of Prague,* Rilke disparages Prague German culture, claiming that its literature has descended to the level of "newspaper scribbling," and he goes on to propose ways of resisting this degradation:

There are only two ways to somehow outlast these circumstances: either to retreat into oneself, to attach oneself more closely to the land, its custom and its charm, as the only intercourse which can support and stabilize . . . or to move abroad, where so many great and promising things are taking place, with a joyful spirit, to appreciate and learn about all things, with the quiet hope in one's heart that one will be able to return to one's homeland having gained expertise, in order to express it in a new and worthy and mature way with words of pure gold.[11]

Rilke was writing about his German-Jewish compatriot, the graphic artist Emil Orlik, but he was surely also thinking of his own situation. Whether or not he nourished, at the time, a hope of someday returning to his homeland, this would never come about. For the rest of his life, Rilke visited old friends and relatives in Prague only reluctantly and infrequently. Yet the remainder of Rilke's statement about Orlik describes his own strategy quite accurately. On the one hand he journeyed out into the wider world, but on the other hand he strove to develop a closer attachment to the customs and inner charm of the Bohemian land. These conflicting desires manifest themselves most obviously in the work he produced during the mid- to late 1890s.

"*Offerings to the Lares*"

Apart from *Two Stories of Prague,* the work that reveals the most about Rilke's exploration of the city's Czech heritage is his collection of ninety poems entitled *Offerings to the Lares.* Published in 1895, this volume of poetry is often associated with *Two Stories of Prague* because of the closeness of date and theme, and Rilke himself once described the Prague stories as "unused residue from *Offerings to the Lares.*"[12] The poems offer much less promise of Rilke's talent than the two novellas and are often clichéd and sentimental; nevertheless they reveal the major images that Rilke associated with his "Lares," or native gods. The young poet's evocation of Prague relies heavily on images

Introduction

of graveyards, twilight, moonlight, stillness, and memory, while he portrays the Czech people as a gentle, subservient race whose finest quality is their attachment to the land and its traditions, an attachment that reveals itself above all in their melancholy folk songs. The places commemorated in *Offerings to the Lares* are the same locales that figure prominently in the Prague stories: the Malá Strana or Lesser Town, the Hradčany or Castle Hill, St. Vitus's Cathedral, the industrial suburb Smíchov, and the Malvazinka graveyard where young children lie buried. In keeping with the graveyard theme, a focus on All Souls' Day and its traditions is common to both works. *Offerings to the Lares* contains a cycle of poems on the tumultuous and tragic events of Czech history that also form the background to *Two Stories of Prague,* including the story of the eccentric and mystical Emperor Rudolph II and the Thirty Years' War, and of Jan Hus, in whose integrity and martyrdom Rilke sees the essence of Czech character, history, and hope for the future.

The overall tone of *Offerings to the Lares* is commemorative; Prague is, for Rilke, a collection of monuments to a melancholy past. The title of the first poem, "My Old House," sounds the keynote of the collection. A related poem, "The House of My Birth," portrays the poet as a dreamy youngster, not unlike Bohush, remembering a blonde girl who lived in the nearby palace of the count. The girl was his childhood companion but has now retreated to a realm of silence — either the grave or, to complete the parallel with Bohush's reminiscence of Aglaya, a convent. Wolfgang Leppmann suggests that this incident may also have a biographical parallel: while Rilke was still in school, he was disturbed by the decision made by his friend and distant relative Amélie to enter a convent. Leppmann suggests that Amélie "lives on as the blond-haired girl in several of his early poems."[13] One of the most famous occurrences of this motif in Rilke's work may be Cornet Christoph Rilke's memory of the blonde girl Magdalena with whom he used to play back home. Coming just after the cornet's recollection of the "old melancholy song" that the girls in the harvest fields used to sing, the incident illustrates the continuity between Rilke's experiences in Prague and his most famous poetry.

Offerings to the Lares, like *Two Stories of Prague,* is the product of a period of transition in Rilke's art, his life-style, and even his personality. The transition is reflected in the fact that many of the poems focus on liminal or "in-between" moments, including twilight, dawn, spring, fall, and the passage from childhood to adulthood, as marked by either a young couple's betrothal or a child's first awareness of death. Projecting his own developmental phase onto the city and its people, Rilke portrays the Czechs as a childish race looking forward to its maturity; its history and tradition always contain a prophecy for the future. Rilke's attitude toward Czech nationalism in *Offerings to the Lares* is strikingly similar to the attitude he adopts in *Two Stories of Prague.* In the poem "Noises of Freedom," he somewhat patronizingly warns the Czech people about the seductive "poets of strife" who are arising among them, and cautions that theirs is not the right way to achieve national independence. Rather, he says, the Czechs should hold to their folk songs and their poetry as an expression of patriotic passion.

In *Two Stories of Prague,* the conception of Czechs as passive and childlike is voiced by King Bohush, the Wanka family, and the young German Ernst Land, characters who have the reader's sympathy and whose voices we may identify to a large extent with Rilke's own. The image of the Czech character that they express corresponds to a Romantic concept reflected in both the literature and politics of the early nineteenth century and shared, at that time, by both Czechs and Germans in Bohemia. Though the inhabitants of Bohemia began increasingly to think of themselves as either Czech or German after the revolutions of 1848, the image of the Czechs as gentle, childlike, and melancholy lingered and had far-reaching effects on the self-image of that ethnic group. By the 1890s, however, the traditional romanticized image was being overwhelmed by rapid changes in the political and cultural constellation of Czech society, some of which Rilke chronicles and criticizes through the intellectuals and radical student groups in his Prague stories. Yet Rilke's acquaintance with Czech nationalism was confined to what went on in literary and artistic, not political, circles. Václav Černý, for one, has argued that Rilke was guilty of a major misassessment of Czech politics in failing to recognize the rapid growth of interest in socialist ideology among the Czechs at the end of the nineteenth century.[14] Despite Rilke's often condescending tone, though, *Offerings to the Lares* was one of the few works by Prague German writers in that era to be acknowledged and praised in the Czech press.[15]

Artists and Intellectuals, Nationalists and Cosmopolitans

Rilke's stories not only engage the history of Prague as a whole, but they are also set in the city's most backward- and inward-looking neighborhood, the Malá Strana, which Rilke knew as Kleinseite and which is usually presented to English visitors as the Lesser Town. The second oldest of the originally separate towns that joined together to form the city of Prague, the Lesser Town is located in the shadow of the Hradčany, or Castle Hill, on the west bank of the Vltava River. It was, at first, dependent on the castle and the aristocratic residences of Hradčany for its livelihood. During the nineteenth century the Lesser Town was known as a charming neighborhood rich in tradition, though most of the actual buildings date back only to the seventeenth or eighteenth century, because the area suffered several fires and had to be largely rebuilt over the course of its history. By Rilke's time, the Lesser Town had acquired the reputation of being not just historical but also backward-looking, steeped in superstition and refusing to admit the existence of the newer town across the Vltava River. Many of its inhabitants were civil servants and office functionaries, or else widows of office workers. This is the Prague from which King Bohush springs and in which the Wanka family seeks refuge when it is forced to leave the country town. By having these characters come into conflict with, and often be victimized and destroyed by, the more modern influences in Prague culture, Rilke exposes some of the internal tensions he sensed as he grew up in the city. His treatment of characters from the Lesser Town reveals a nostalgia for the mystical tradition that the place represents, and also a recognition that if its inhabitants are not to be destroyed by modern city life, as Bohush and Zdenko Wanka are, then they must compromise and enter into a relationship with it, as Luisa does and as Rilke himself did.

The ambiguity in Rilke's attitude toward the backwardness of the Lesser Town is exemplified by the character of Bohush. With a deformed body but the sensibility of a poet, Bohush illustrates the author's conception of the true Czech character. He spends his days working at a tedious and poorly paid job, his evenings at home with his elderly mother, his Sundays walking in the cemetery with the mysterious woman he imagines is his girlfriend. His life is wretched, yet he manages to find a simple, natural pleasure in the coming of spring, in religious rites, in companionship and conversation.

The antagonists of Bohush, the avant-garde literati who gather in the National Café, are less complex characters, yet the representation of this group is one of the most intriguing aspects of "King Bohush." Rilke manages to both satirize the artists as a group and bring out their individual characteristics and idiosyncrasies. We know that the actor Norinski is a haughty windbag; the journalist Karás is a tall, thin caricature of the intellectual and the most pretentious member of the group; the novelist Pátek is a fastidious and fickle dandy; Machal is a dreamy poet who has trouble staying in touch with reality; the artist Schileder, the most sympathetic of the lot (who has, interestingly, the most German-sounding name), is compassionate, conciliatory, and insecure about his own ability to fit in with the crowd. Together, they present a cross section of the different trends in avant-garde Czech culture in the 1890s, and they contrast as a group with Rezek, the student who associates with them but is characterized from the beginning as a loner who sits off to the side and drinks in silence.

Behind the debates of the National Café crowd lies an actual struggle that went on between two schools of Czech writers, the nationalists or Ruchovci, led by Svatopluk Čech, with their journal *Ruch,* and the cosmopolitans or Lumírovci who published the weekly journal *Lumír.* In their attempt to westernize Czech art, the latter group welcomed influences not only from France but also from Italy, England, and Spain, as well as Russia and parts of Asia. Rilke is critical of the cosmopolitans, whom he characterizes as impatient and imitative, unwilling to allow a true national culture to develop and overeager to import the latest trends from Paris. The essay Rilke published in 1900 on Emil Orlik confirms Rilke's belief that Czech culture suffered from its susceptibility to French influence; in that essay he refers to Czech culture as "a profound and intimate art" that is developing "with a good rising generation, only one that is somewhat strongly influenced by the French."[16] The same opinion is vehemently expounded by the student Rezek in both of the Prague stories. Once again, however, Rilke's anti-French bias seems to indicate that he is representing the literary and cultural situation more accurately than the political reality. As Peter Demetz points out, Rezek's bitter denunciation of Parisian influence is implausible; as a Slavic patriot, Rezek would be more likely to regard Paris as sacrosanct, since a Franco-Russian alliance had been concluded in 1891.[17]

Both the nationalistic and cosmopolitan schools resisted the trends set by the newest and most avant-garde group of Czech writers, the decadents led by Jiří Karásek ze Lvovic (1871–1951). Influenced by the French symbolist movement, these poets and reviewers gravitated toward themes of worldweariness, eroticism, and death, and published in Arnošt Procházka's monthly *Moderní Revue.* Karásek ze Lvovic, an acquaintance of Rilke's, is alluded to in Rilke's choice of the name Karás for his cosmopolitan critic and reviewer. Rezek's denunciation of modern poets who retreat into medievalism and orientalism also seems directed at Karásek ze Lvovic's work.

The names of other characters in "King Bohush" contain allusions to well-known literary and academic figures in nineteenth-century Prague. The lyric poet Machal recalls Karel Hynek Mácha (1810–1836), a tragically short-lived Romantic poet whose major achievement, a long Byronic poem entitled "May," seems alluded to in the major speech that Rilke gives Machal in "King Bohush." At the same time, Machal's ambivalent relationship to Czech patriotism links him with Josef Svatopluk Machar (1864–1942), a contemporary of Rilke's whose political poetry both supported and attacked the Czech nationalist movement, since he insisted on a highly personal expression of his nationalistic sentiments. "Rezek" was the name of a historian and professor of Czech history at Prague's Czech University. The name, appropriately for one of the most important and ambiguous characters, and the only one who appears in both stories, suggests allusions that lead in several directions. A nickname meaning redhead or rusty, Rezek is indicative of the character's hot temper and his striking, eccentric appearance. Perhaps it may not be going too far to mention the similarity with the biblical Judas, traditionally considered a red-haired man; this brings out an element of Christian martyrdom in the character of Bohush that is surely in keeping with the religious overtones of the story. By giving Rezek the name of an academic who specialized in Czech history, Rilke also points to his nationalistic allegiance and recalls the fact that a professor, Antonín Čížek, was at one time suspected of committing the actual murder on which the story of Bohush is based.

The most colorful of the society crowd in "King Bohush," the actor Norinski, is probably a caricature of František Krumlovský (1817–1875), renowned in Bohemia not only as a tragic actor but also as a haunting Byronic figure. Tall, athletic, with a striking face and an ability to convey intense emotion, Krumlovský had an almost hypnotic effect on his audiences when

Introduction

performing, while off the stage he was known for his rootless and dissipated life-style. Though his strong personality led people to associate him with brave Czech nationalists, and though he was a friend of the Czech literary hero Josef Kajetán Tyl, Krumlovský usually performed in German in the theaters of Vienna. The conflict between art and politics, or between Czech nationalism and German theater, is reflected in the character of Norinski, who proudly gives the lie to anyone who suggests he might not be a true Czech patriot, yet just as disdainfully spurns Bohush, Rilke's representative of the enduring Czech spirit. Norinski's most significant pronouncement on nationalism in art comes in his reaction to Karás's review of his performance in *Hamlet,* a scene that strongly supports the identification with Krumlovský, who also appeared in that play. Norinski's insistence on an interpretation of Hamlet taken "directly from the English" alludes to developments in Czech literature in the 1890s, an era when cosmopolitan writers were interested in making Western classics available to Czech readers, and when both Josef Václav Sládek and his friend Jaroslav Vrchlický completed translations of Shakespeare for the Czech theater.[18]

Rilke weaves these satirical portraits of his contemporaries and near contemporaries together with the historical account of an actual murder to create "King Bohush," a text that is more closely connected with current events than any other piece of writing he produced. Once again, it is remarkable that Rilke not only made use of contemporary politics but also specifically based his story on events within the Czech community. The germ of the plot is a murder that took place in the Lesser Town in 1893 and culminated in a sensational trial that became known throughout Bohemia. Among the Czech cultural-political organizations that sprang up at the end of the nineteenth century was one called Omladina (Youth), with which a paperhanger named Rudolf Mrva was associated. Mrva was described in newspaper reports as a hunchback with an eccentric, romantic temperament. After he was found to have betrayed the organization to the Austrian police, he was strangled and stabbed to death in his widowed mother's apartment shortly before Christmas in 1893. Two members of Omladina, the painter F. Dragouna and the locksmith O. Doležal, were charged with his murder. The local details of this incident find their way into both of Rilke's Prague stories: Mrva lived, like Bohush, at 13 Bridge Street (Brückengasse or Mostecká) in the Lesser Town; he was buried, like Zdenko, in the Olšany cemetery; the National Café and the Vikárka pub are actual locales in which the political intrigues occurred. A recent critic, Helmut Naumann, points out that the first name of Rudolf Mrva is subtly present in Bohush's praise of the House of Artists or "Rudolphinum," and in the fact that the single date mentioned in "King Bohush," April 17, is the name day dedicated to the medieval martyr Rudolph, whose epithet is "the childlike."[19]

However sensational the Omladina trial was, Rilke's story goes far beyond the dramatization of a newspaper account. Unlike Mrva, Bohush is innocent of the treachery with which Rezek charges him, or at worst he unintentionally betrays the revolutionary group out of a pathetically misplaced sense of heroism and nationalistic fervor. Rilke turns what was originally a case of political intrigue and infighting into a study of character, exploring in detail the psychology and motivations of Bohush as well as the differences in ideology and personality among the Czech nationalists. And if Bohush himself represents the aspect of the Czech character that Rilke believes will eventually mature into a strong, sensitive, culturally rich race, the fate of Bohush dramatizes what the coffeehouse debates suggest in a more subdued, parodic manner: Rilke's conviction that the more aggressive and hate-centered elements in the nationalistic movement are actually destroying what is valuable in the culture they mean to promote. Bohush, like Zdenko Wanka, not only voices the author's opinions on which aspects of the Czech spirit are pure and noble, but he also becomes a personification of the suffering Czech people, under attack even by their own would-be champions.

"King Bohush"

In "King Bohush," Rilke's perspective on Czech nationalism emerges from the conversation and conflict between Bohush and Rezek. Different as they are, the two agree on a central point: Czech artists should allow the national culture to develop along its own lines and not go chasing after foreign influences and subject matter. But Rezek is ready with sarcastic denunciations of the cosmopolitan artists and would compel them to write about Czech history and Czech themes, while to Bohush the choice of subject matter is not really important so long as artists are faithful to the spirit of the Czech people. It is the uneducated Bohush, rather than the revolutionary student Rezek, who truly cares about the poverty and oppression of Czech workers and wants to see their condition represented in Czech art. Rezek would compel a nationalistic art by taking themes from the nation's past, while Bohush wants art to be a natural expression of the people's present circumstances.

The opinion of Bohush agrees with Rilke's own belief, apparent from other texts, that the most sincere manifestation of Czech culture is in the folk songs that spring from people's lips as they work on the land. The ideal of a spontaneous, natural art is emphasized by the recurring image of springtime and blossoming in "King Bohush" which the poet Machal introduces in his monologue in the opening scene:

"Just look outside. This fight against the stupid, un-ploughed clods, that each of the delicate, frail seeds must fight in order to reach its summer. Here," and he wriggled up a bit higher, "stands the helpless blossom wanting to bloom; that's the single thing she can do, she can only bloom, and she really doesn't want to disturb anyone, and yet they are all against her: the black topsoil, that lets her through only after lengthy pleading, the days that scatter warmth and rain and wind indiscriminately down on her, and the nights that creep up on her slowly in order to strangle her with their icy fingers. This cowardly, wretched fight, this is spring."

Machal's diatribe against spring is not the babbling of a man out of touch with the political issues that the others around him are discussing. Rather, this passage may provide the truest expression of Rilke's political philosophy. Machal directs his listeners to "just look outside," where a policeman, a representative of the Austrian state apparatus, happens to be passing up and down in front of the Czech theater; while Machal thinks that is not exactly what he wanted to point out to anyone, perhaps it is a more appropriate analogy than he realizes for what he has to say. He describes a helpless bud fighting to attain its natural development in the face of opposition from the more powerful clods of soil and the tyranny of adverse weather, an image which we may take to represent the Czech people in their struggle against the more powerful Germans. Rezek echoes the same image when he speaks, a few pages later, of the "long, lonely way through oppression" that the nation must find, of the "new, timid strength of a beginning" that "wells up in its veins," even of its "springtime." Significantly, as Rezek says this, there is again a policeman standing by, glancing suspiciously in his direction.

Bohush, with his faith in the Czech people, feels the story of the cruel spring as an affront against both his experience of the natural world and the quiet perseverence of his race. Immediately after Machal's speech he attempts to defend the spring — but in trying to support the budding flower of Czech culture he becomes like it and finds himself overpowered by his environment, unable to rise up and assert himself. Given the importance of this image of budding and growth, it is significant that the story takes place in the spring — beginning, to be exact, on April 17. For a city as far north as Prague, mid-April is still, as Rilke stresses, only early spring. In cultural terms, the setting seems to indicate Rilke's belief that Czech culture is beginning to bud, though it is as yet only in the preliminary stages of growth. Conversely, during Bohush's bewildered wandering through the streets of Prague in the penultimate scene of the novella, the fact that he can no longer recognize the signs of spring or morning is an indication of how confused he has become through his association with Rezek, and how alienated from the true nature of the Czech people.

If the influence of nationalism on art is the most realistic aspect of "King Bohush," the other extreme of romanticism is represented by the female roles in the story. Rilke's imagination reaches from young female revolutionaries to fairy-tale themes of faithless beloveds and a beautiful maiden shut up forever in the strictest of convents. The characters Frantishka, Carla, Aglaya, and Bohush's mother are not overly original or subtle, but their symbolic roles are significant. If Frantishka represents an erotic relationship and Aglaya a mystical, religious one, the mysterious Carla, apparently Frantishka's younger sister, combines the two. She first appears in Bohush's dream as a young girl in a nun's habit who declares her love for Bohush, and she is later revealed to be centrally involved in Rezek's revolutionary society. As saint, desperate lover, and fervent revolutionary, she seems to offer everything Bohush could want — and yet we are given some reason to doubt whether she really exists at all. She is only glimpsed in a feverish dream and in a dim cellar where Bohush hears her declaring, improbably, "I love him so." It may be that he has imagined recognizing her just as he must have imagined the words he longs to hear coming from her lips. Perhaps it is more likely that she — and, to some extent, every female figure in the story — is a projection of Bohush's image, and Rilke's image, of the ideal Slavic woman. The most memorable features of these female characters are those on which Rilke typically focuses in his representation of women: Carla's expressive hands; Frantishka's sad eyes that are like a dark, quiet wood; Aglaya's golden laughter; and old Mrs. Bohush's maternal love.

With the possible exception of Bohush's mother, the only real function of the women in the story is to reject the hunchback, and it is after his beloved and then his saint abandons him that Bohush turns to nationalism as the only cause left in which to invest his strength. This suggests that Rilke, who is clearly uncomfortable with organized political movements, considers such movements a perverted form of patriotic expression to which people are driven by too much suffering and neglect. Only when Bohush is distracted by sleeplessness and suffering does he begin to think of storming churches and palaces as an appropriate expression of national feeling. The proper and natural course for the Czech spirit, Rilke suggests, is the hateless patriotism that Bohush affirmed earlier, which is willing to share the land with another ethnic group and declines to hate because "hate makes one so sad."

Bohush never completely gives up this belief, and one should remember that he does get to make his coveted speech, albeit in the highly ironic closing lines of the story. His message is that artists should write and paint the people and tell them they are beautiful. While saying this, Bohush himself becomes "beautiful" as he falls asleep and the lines of tension and age fade from his face. But far from speechifying in front of a crowd of revolutionaries, he hasn't, in fact, spoken to anyone; his message becomes a secret he will never betray. Hence the bitter irony: Rezek murders him because he believes Bohush *has* betrayed the cause. Rilke, who favored surprise endings, especially in his early work, achieves a double twist here: the sudden murder of Bohush, and the fact that Bohush has uttered the secret of Czech spirit and patriotism, even though no one but the reader is aware of it. Rezek, with his threatening "Did you keep quiet?" may have the last word, but he doesn't know the answer to his own question; Bohush has spoken out, only not as a traitor but as a true Czech.

"The Siblings"

"The Siblings" overlaps with "King Bohush" in terms of setting and theme; Rezek is a central character in both stories, and "The Siblings" takes place during the time of increased ethnic tension that follows the Bohush incident. Yet it is a different type of story: more lyrical, less cohesive, more extreme, and therefore less realistic in plot and characterization. If the setting is less convincing than in "King Bohush," this may be because Rilke was far less familiar with the life of lower-middle-class Czech apartment dwellers than with the intellectual coffeehouse life-style he describes in the earlier story. Yet this shift in perspective gives us a more objective view of the Czech intellectuals, as we see them through the eyes of Zdenko, a spiritual outsider and a newcomer to Prague. The result is a more serious criticism of the artistic elite; the National Café crowd now appears tired and testy, grasping for a sense of purpose by means of an exaggerated and artificial rhetorical exertion. Zdenko Wanka, even more obviously than Bohush, must force himself to regard his own people as the politically oppressed race that the revolutionary intellectuals insist they are. It is one more strong indication that Rilke believes the organized nationalistic movement is inconsistent with the experiences of genuine Czech people, whether they are from the countryside or the heart of Prague.

The characteristic imagery of "The Siblings" is one of up and down, higher and lower, as introduced by Zdenko's literally "revolutionary" tale about how the social order is really the inverse of what one usually imagines it to be. Ordinary people, he claims, are really at the top, while God, priest, and king are at the bottom:

"It seems to me that very deep down is the Good Lord and a little over him the pope and so forth. But at the top are the people. Only the people are not one, they are many; they push and shove one another, and one of them eclipses the sun for someone else. So I always think they should lift someone or other up to a height from time to time, not too high (he could easily fall down to where the king is, or the emperor), but still so that he feels their strong and loyal shoulders under him and can look out over their heads for a while in quiet reflection."

The image is picked up again several times in a political or ideological context, in Zdenko's attempt to regard his intellectual friends as being "at the summit of the race," in the revolutionary students' attempt to "lift" Zdenko "above the law of equality" that reigns within the cemetery walls, in Mrs. Wanka's admonition to Luisa that she must aim "higher up" than the position of a servant or shop girl. Physical versions of the same theme appear in the treacherous narrow staircase that winds up through the Wankas' apartment building, in the new grave that holds Zdenko's body, in the tower in Krumlov castle from which the maiden in blue jumps to her death, and in the grisly legend of the deep dungeon in the Hunger Tower, or Daliborka. Prague appears as the "great city with its many abysses," a phrase that is particularly apt for this story in which the typical experiences are those of being lost in a crowd; being confined alone in a room, a prison cell, or a dungeon; and jumping or falling from a tower into a black abyss.

These experiences link the mythical past of Prague and Bohemia with its present reality, often by way of Rilke's own experience. In March 1895 Rilke visited the town of Krumlov (in German, Krummau) in southern Bohemia, saw the castle with its famous ballroom, and heard the legend about the young woman who threw herself from the tower room to escape being raped by the emperor's wild son. The legend reappears in one of the most extended neoromantic segments in "The Siblings," and the girl in the blue dress becomes a foil for Luisa. If Luisa's girlhood is haunted by the erotic vision of Prince Julius Caesar pursuing her into the tower, her transition to adulthood is signaled by the reversal of roles in the story: she imagines herself trying to push her attacker from the tower, then pulling him to her in a rush of passion. Luisa's development from a powerless Czech girl into a capable woman who helps draw the cultures together is emphasized through the contrast with the anonymous maiden of Bohemian legend. Rezek's story of the St. Wenceslas prison functions in a parallel but more tragic way. St. Wenceslas is the patron saint of Bohemia, but here his name serves only to designate an institution that confines Czech prisoners. The derelict penitentiary, its walls still eloquent with cries of desperation, foreshadows other deserted buildings that haunt Rilke's work, such as the exposed inner walls of half-demolished apartments that appear in *Malte Laurids Brigge.*

The familial situations in "The Siblings" and "King Bohush" are parallel, and their similarity serves to bring out elements latent in both stories. Both tell of strong, stern fathers who have died before the story begins — not only the elder Bohush and Mr. Wanka, two honorable servants of the German aristocracy, but also the domineering father of Ernst Land. The vacuum created by the deaths of these men leaves widows and children to overcome a sense of emptiness and loss, and to find their own way in life. Yet there is also an undeniable element of relief and release in the death of patriarchal figures which may well reflect Rilke's own experience; though he did not lose his father, in leaving Prague in 1896 the young writer had finally broken free of parental interference in his chosen life-style. In "The Siblings" there is an especially strong sense that death is followed by a brief period of loss and mourning, which soon gives way to a new-found energy and sense of purpose. This is Zdenko's experience in regard to his father's death, Mrs. Wanka's experience when Zdenko dies, and finally Luisa's experience when she loses her mother. The understanding of loss as the impetus for a new, energetic approach to life has its basis in the major transitions that Rilke himself was living through at the time.

Sociologically, "The Siblings" is about a typical Czech family in which the parents have spent their lives as domestic servants to German aristocrats, and Luisa and Mrs. Meering von Meerhelm both reveal an unthinking expectation that the next generation will do the same. But this family has higher goals for its children: Mrs. Wanka leaves her home, moves to Prague, and makes endless sacrifices so that her son can study to become a doctor, and she directs her daughter into a course of study that will qualify her for the higher position of governess. Luisa's budding success at the end of the story implies the author's support for this liberalistic approach toward a change of status for Czech workers.

In a different sense from "King Bohush," this story is also about the coming of age of a people. Political and personal development is contained within the story of the Czech girl Luisa, whose emergence into womanhood parallels the elevation of her social status as she becomes a mistress and landlady — "Miss Wanka" — at the end of the story. Like the female characters in "King Bohush," Luisa embodies the qualities of an ideal woman, not least because of her Czech heritage. Slavic softness seems to be the necessary moderating influence in the lonely life of Ernst Land, whose name literally means "earnest land" or "stern country." According to Peter Demetz, the relationship between a German man, often a student, and a Czech girl (in whom Demetz finds a symbol for the dark, seductive city of Prague) was a common theme in German novels of the period.[20] "The Siblings" makes use of this theme twice: Land's relationship with Luisa repeats the relationship between his own Czech mother and German father.

Introduction

"The Siblings" substantiates Bohush's belief — or Rilke's belief, expressed through Bohush — that genuine Czech culture consists in the folk songs and legends of the people as well as in the natural self-expression of contemporary Czechs, immature, uneducated, and poor as they are. This story introduces an opposition between the rural town of Krumlov and the capital, Prague, as well as between the time of the Thirty Years' War and Rilke's own day. Yet these oppositions evolve into parallels, most obviously in the scene in which Zdenko and Rezek find themselves at the half-demolished St. Wenceslas Prison. Its eerie, graffiti-covered walls are a pathetic parody of the fantastically painted walls of the ballroom at Krumlov Castle, just as the later visit to the deep pit in the Daliborka recalls the tower at Krumlov Castle, both places threatening a fatal fall. Although Zdenko sneers at his sister's timidity with regard to the Krumlov legend, he has a similarly nervous reaction to the St. Wenceslas penitentiary: in both cases the figures on the walls threaten to come alive and overwhelm the intruder, forcing him or her to relive a bygone horror. The implied comparison between the artistry of the Krumlov walls, painted centuries before with consummate skill by (Rilke claims) a French artist, and the crude but expressive scratches made by a recent generation of Czech prisoners, is emphasized by Rezek's sardonic observation that the St. Wenceslas walls should be preserved as a national treasure. Later, in the pub, Rezek observes that there is a similarity between their own time and the days before the Thirty Years' War in the early seventeenth century, a comment that his listeners find strangely unsettling. Perhaps he has only spoken aloud their suspicion that the Czech people are haunted by their own past and must still go through violent upheavals in the slow process of maturation.

Yet a fruitful maturity is the promise of the story's closing pages, which again are set in the auspicious season of early spring. The sudden transformation of Luisa, within days of her mother's death, from a nervous child into a confident, independent, professional woman ready to break with convention by sharing her apartment with a single German man, seems overly idealistic and insufficiently motivated. Still, it is true to Rilke's own spiritual development in the months before he wrote *Two Stories of Prague*. The empowerment he gained by living independently and supporting himself at least in part by his writing is reflected in Luisa's new-found status as music teacher and manager of a household. His escape from the confinement of Prague into the wider world is hinted at in Luisa's spontaneous dash through the streets of the Lesser Town, and her admonition to Ernst Land to stop playing the mole and come outside to enjoy the spring. Her developing relationship with Land is subtly suggestive of the discreet but unconventional affair Rilke had recently begun with Lou Andreas-Salomé. Finally, the young couple's decision to learn each other's language is a concluding reminder of Prague's problems as well as a harbinger of Rilke's future cosmopolitanism. The Prague stories end with a new sense of communication between German and Czech, a situation that represents Rilke's idealistic, liberal solution to the sterile separation of the two cultures in Prague, as well as the perspective of a pan-European poet still searching for his true homeland.

Neoromanticism and Naturalism

In terms of style, the *Two Stories of Prague* are again emblematic of a phase of development that culminated in the tone and imagery of Rilke's mature prose. In his detailed stylistic study of Rilke's prose, Kurt Rothmann repeatedly refers to the period beginning in 1897 as a time when Rilke's writing underwent an evolution from a "descriptive early style" to a "more meditative late style."[21] Hallmarks of this evolution are an increase in the number of adjectives Rilke used and a decrease in the number of nouns, the frequent use of the conjunction *and*, and a tendency to use *it* as the subject of a sentence. Features like these reflect the fact that mood is becoming more important than plot in Rilke's prose: thus verbs are often intransitive, reflexive, or copula, and present and imperfect tenses are preferred over the perfect, giving the impression that little action is taking place and temporality is suspended.

The latent lyricism in *Two Stories of Prague* was recognized early, well before it came to fruition in *Malte Laurids Brigge* or Rilke's later poetry. In a review that appeared in a German periodical early in 1901, Hans Bethge highlights the quality of "sweet reminiscence" in the stories and their evocation of the magical, haunting character of Prague's churches and palaces. He goes on to say that this lyrical quality is so obviously the most effective aspect of the stories that the narrative might as well be omitted: "The events in the book are completely insignificant, and they might as well be entirely absent. We are dealing solely with two lyrical moods, and with the sensitive sketches of a romantic dreamer, in whom naïveté and decadent stirrings . . . are combined in an unusual way. We've known for a long time that Rilke was a true lyric artist."[22]

The tension between realistic narrative and the long lyrical passages that often threaten to overwhelm the plot is due in part to Rilke's experimentation with two widely differing literary movements during the 1890s. The shift from a neo-romanticism reminiscent of Heinrich Heine to a naturalism that is a belated echo of work being produced in Berlin, particularly by the young Gerhart Hauptmann, is most apparent in Rilke's plays of this period. Between 1895 and 1897 Rilke developed a sudden and short-lived interest in naturalistic drama, especially in the work of Rudolf Christoph Jenny. In their English translation of Rilke's early plays, Klaus Phillips and John Locke attribute this infatuation to the fact that Prague's two German theaters suddenly, in 1895, began producing plays by modern playwrights after years of confining themselves to the classics.[23]

Rilke's concern with social problems during the mid-1890s is evident not only from the subject and style of his dramas, but also from the way he chose to circulate his poetry during this period. He composed a journal entitled *Wegwarten* (*Chi-*

cory Flowers), printed it in his apartment, and handed out free copies to institutions such as hospitals and even to passersby on street corners. Ironically, though, he failed to reach the lower classes who were his intended audience, for he was literally writing in the wrong language — German — while the large majority of Prague's poorer inhabitants were Czech. Rilke's sincere but awkwardly handled concern for creating an art that spoke to and about the condition of oppression and poverty is equally apparent from his publishing efforts, his plays, and the often unconvincing naturalism of his Prague stories.

Achieving the Past

Anticipating his later aversion to having his early work remembered and reprinted, Rilke referred slightingly to *Two Stories of Prague* in letters to friends and acquaintances, even during and shortly after the publication of the volume. What is interesting about his references, though, is that they inevitably treat the stories as a way of comprehending and relating to the past, by which Rilke meant primarily his own childhood. Immediately after the publication of *Two Stories of Prague,* on 8 September 1899, he sent a copy of the volume to Tolstoy, whom he had met a few months earlier on his first trip to Russia. His accompanying letter stressed the Slavic environment in which Rilke had grown up: "I enclose a small book, which grew out of many dark sentiments that bind me to my Slavic homeland, Prague."[24]

While in Russia in early 1899, Rilke reflected on the stories he had recently completed, and wrote an advertisement for the volume. In that brief notice Rilke acknowledges the extent to which he has personalized the political:

> The aim of this book was to somehow come closer to my own childhood. For all art longs to grow richer by that vanished garden, its perfumes and its darknesses, to become more eloquent by its murmurs. The pretext was

just two little stories. Prague, that city full of dark alleys and mysterious courtyards, is the setting. The characters, who seldom act, are dreamy and melancholy. Slavic longing lies in their voices and they live on the ready piety of their unspent feelings. And so by means of the pretext something new came in: the story of the childhood of a race. A few words tell in passing of the destiny of a race which cannot spread forth its childhood alongside the older, serious, grown-up brother race. And it seems to me now that my book's greatest worth lies in these words spoken aloud almost by chance. For all its warmth comes from there; and precisely where it seems to grow tendentious it grows wide and wise and human.[25]

Rilke locates the value of his stories in their evocation of the childhood of a race, yet this element of political philosophy is literally situated between the personal — the writer's desire to remember and comprehend his own chidhood — and the human, the realm in which all political aspects of his stories come to rest. The development of the Czech people becomes a way of illustrating the writer's own fashioning of himself into an adult; once this is accomplished, the political recedes, and virtually all of Rilke's prose written from that point on concentrates on what is "wide and wise and human." Despite the elements of naturalism in the Prague stories, the evocation of the dead-end lives of poverty-stricken Czechs like Bohush and his mother or the Wanka family, and the realism in the depiction of the coffeehouse literati, Rilke's interest in describing social and political conditions is always vying with, and usually giving way to, his interest in the lyrical and personal.

In his foreword to *Two Stories of Prague,* Rilke again emphasizes that the book brought him closer to his own childhood: "This book is nothing but the past. Homeland and childhood — both long since remote — are its background. I would not have written it *this* way today, and therefore would probably not have written it at all . . . It has made half-forgotten things dear to me and made me a present of them." Rilke overstates his own distance from the stories and from the experience that lies behind them. The idea that his homeland and childhood were "long since remote" and that "today" he would have written the stories differently or not at all is countered by the reality that the twenty-three-year-old Rilke had finished writing the novellas only a few months earlier, and had been away from Prague for all of a year and a half. The foreword gives an impression of how rapidly Rilke felt he was changing, and how desperately he wanted to progress in his career.

Despite Rilke's decision to leave Prague permanently and his frequent repudiation of his background, those who knew him and those who study his work repeatedly affirm the importance of Prague and Bohemian culture to his beliefs and writings. Willy Lorenz writes, "Whoever knows Bohemia and whoever knows Rilke will soon reach the conclusion that this land was virtually personified in the poet's life and forms the foundation of his work and that from this perspective much in the life and achievement of the poet becomes comprehensible."[26] Among the aspects of Rilke's character that Lorenz identifies as Bohemian (that is, Czech) are his affection for Russia and Paris as well as for historical tradition, his penchant for the conditions of suffering and of indolence, and his relationship to Christianity. J.-F. Angelloz, Rilke's first biographer, adds to the list Rilke's taste for old buildings and unusual people, his attraction to a fantastic, ghostly world, and the musicality of his language.[27]

Pointing out that Prague was the only city to which Rilke addressed poetry, and the Czechs the only people he tried to analyze as a race, Peter Demetz concludes that the experience of Prague and Bohemia was the dominant experience of Rilke's childhood and the most important formative factor in his life: "Rilke's life and work are, far more

Introduction

than it may seem from his own claims, determined by his personal response to the challenge of the place and time of his origins. In his youth in Prague . . . he makes his choice, which leads the way into his future existence."[28] Thus encouraged, we may read the stories that represent Rilke's response to the experience of Prague both to discover the continuities between his origins and his later work, and to appreciate the extent to which what Rilke says of the heroes of his stories, Bohush and Zdenko, might also be said of the writer himself: namely, that *"er ist ein anderer geworden"* — he has become a different person.

Endnotes

1. *Letters of Rainer Maria Rilke*, vol. 2, *1910–1926*, trans. Jane Bannard Greene and M. D. Herter Norton (New York: Norton, 1948), 274.
2. J. F. Hendry, *The Sacred Threshold: A Life of Rainer Maria Rilke* (Manchester: Carcanet, 1983); Wolfgang Leppmann, *Rilke: A Life*, trans. Wolfgang Leppmann and Russell M. Stockman (New York: Fromm International, 1984); Donald Prater, *A Ringing Glass: The Life of Rainer Maria Rilke* (Oxford: Clarendon, 1986.)
3. Carl Sieber, *René Rilke* (Leipzig: Insel, 1932); Peter Demetz, *René Rilkes Prager Jahre* (Düsseldorf: Eugen Diederichs, 1953).
4. Demetz, *René Rilkes Prager Jahre*, 11.
5. Leppmann, *Rilke*, 89–90.
6. Gary B. Cohen, *The Politics of Ethnic Survival: Germans in Prague, 1861–1914* (Princeton, N.J.: Princeton Univ. Press, 1981), 137.
7. Václav Černý, *Rainer Maria Rilke, Prag, Böhmen und die Tschechen*, trans. Jaromír Povejšil and Gitta Wolfová (Artia, 1966), 9.
8. Clara Mágr, "Sprach Rilke tschechisch?" *Blätter der Rilke-Gesellschaft* 13 (1986), 83–92.
9. Joachim W. Storck, "Rilke als Staatsbürger der Tschechoslowakischen Republik," *Blätter der Rilke-Gesellschaft* 13 (1986), 39–54.
10. Rio Preisner, "Rilke in Böhmen: Kritische Prolegomena zum alt-neuen Thema," *Rilke Heute: Beziehungen und Wirkungen*, ed. Ingeborg H. Solbrig und Joachim W. Storck (Frankfurt a.M.: Suhrkamp, 1975), 213.
11. Rilke, "Ein Prager Künstler," *Ver Sacrum* 7 (1 April 1900); reprinted in *Zwei Prager Geschichten und Ein Prager Künstler*, ed. Josef Mühlberger (Frankfurt a.M.: Insel, 1976), 139.

Introduction

12. Letter to Wilhelm von Scholz, 10 April 1899, *Gesammelte Briefe,* vol. 1, *Briefe aus den Jahren 1892 bis 1904,* ed. Ruth Sieber-Rilke and Carl Sieber (Leipzig: Insel, 1939).

13. Leppmann, *Rilke,* 26.

14. Černý, *Rainer Maria Rilke, Prag, Böhmen und die Tschechen,* 37.

15. Václav Černý, "Noch einmal und anders: Rilke und die Tschechen," trans. Christian Tuschinsky, *Die Welt der Slaven* 22 (1977).

16. Rilke, "Ein Prager Künstler," 139.

17. Demetz, *René Rilkes Prager Jahre,* 157.

18. I am indebted to Marcela Moc for suggesting the identification for Norinski and for translating accounts of Krumlovský from Czech sources.

19. Helmut Naumann, *Studien zu Rilkes frühem Werk* (Berlin: Schäuble, 1991), 66.

20. Demetz, *René Rilkes Prager Jahre,* 102.

21. Kurt K. F. Rothmann, "Die Stilentwicklung in Rilkes dichterischer Prosa" (Ph.D. diss., Univ. of Cincinnati, 1966), 13.

22. Hans Bethge, review of *Zwei Prager Geschichten, Stimmen der Gegenwart* (February 1901): 79.

23. *Nine Plays,* trans. Klaus Phillips and John Locke (New York: Ungar, 1979), x.

24. Letter to Leo Tolstoy, 8 September 1899, *Briefe in Zwei Bänden,* vol. 1, *1896 bis 1919,* ed. Horst Nalewski (Frankfurt a.M.: Insel, 1991).

25. Rilke, "Selbstanzeige: Zwei Prager Geschichten," in *Sämtliche Werke,* ed. Ernst Zinn, 6 vols. (Frankfurt a.M.: Insel, 1955–1966), vol. 6, 1210.

26. Willy Lorenz, "Rainer Maria Rilke und Böhmen," *Die Furche* (Vienna: Albrecht Dürer, 1947), 292.

27. J.-F. Angelloz, *Rainer Maria Rilke: Leben und Werk,* trans. Alfred Kuoni (Zürich: Arche, 1955), 51.

28. Demetz, *René Rilkes Prager Jahre,* 6–7.

Two
Stories of
Prague

FOREWORD

THIS BOOK is nothing but the past. Homeland and childhood — both long since remote — are its background. I would not have written it *this* way today, and therefore would probably not have written it at all. But at the time I wrote it, it was essential to me. It has made half-forgotten things dear to me and made me a present of them; for we possess only that part of the past which we love. And we want to possess all we have experienced.

SCHMARGENDORF, February 1899
Rainer Maria Rilke

King Bohush

WHEN THE GREAT ACTOR NORINSKI entered the National Café, which is located in front of Prague's Czech Theater,[1] at three o'clock in the afternoon, he started a little — but then immediately smiled his most disdainful smile. The mirror diagonally opposite the door had caught some remote corner of the room, and in it he had recognized a crooked marble column, and underneath this column a small hunchbacked man, whose peculiar eyes, as if in ambush, stared at him out of a misshapen head as he entered. The strangeness of this gaze, in the depths of which some unheard-of event seemed dimly mirrored, had for a moment put him in fright. Not that he was particularly fearful by nature — rather, it was a consequence of the profound and pensive character that is usually inherent in such great artists, like a bulwark, which every action must penetrate. Norinski felt nothing of the sort toward the original. In fact, he overlooked the hunchback for quite a while as he extended his hand with unnecessary pomp to the others at the table of regulars. The handshakes demanded a fair amount of time, since each one apparently comprised three acts. First act: the performer's hand responds languidly to the pleas of the outstretched hands. Second act: his hand says emphatically to the one it clasps, "Do you, too, mark the significance of this moment?" Third act and catastrophe, in which Norinski disdainfully let go of every hand, tossed it away: "Oh, you poor wretch, of course you can't feel it at all . . ." The poor wretches, in this case, were Karás, the tall, pale critic for the

1. The National Theater, on Národní třída (Ferdinandstrasse) near the Vltava River, was built between 1868 and 1881 in the neo-Renaissance style. After its initial construction, it was completely destroyed by fire on 12 August 1881. When the government in Vienna refused financial support, it was reconstructed with donations from Czech citizens and with the participation of most of the leading artists of the time, and it became a symbol of the rebirth of Czech culture.

The National Café is the Café Slavia opposite the National Theater, constructed in 1861 to 1863 as the Lažan Palace. It is a traditional meeting place for writers and artists.

Czas,[2] distinguished by an exceedingly long neck and (as a malicious Jewish colleague had once declared) an exceedingly polite Adam's apple, which accompanied every drop through the solitude of the throat as far as the edge of the collar, where it could no longer lose its way, and from there hurried back to its post, eager to serve; Schileder, the handsome painter, who painted such melancholy things; the novelist Pátek; the lyric poet Machal; and the student Rezek, who sat slightly off to the side, drinking hot *czay* with plenty of cognac out of a large glass, in silence. Finally Norinski seemed to notice the hunchback as well. He laughed, "King Bohush!"[3] and, with an ironic "Your Majesty," reached his hand across the marble table. The little man jumped up, and, so as not to keep the actor's hand waiting, advanced his yellow, undersize fingers too hastily, so that the two hands chased one another like birds in the air. To Bohush this seemed rather comical and he let out a trembling, broken laugh, which he nervously cut short when he noticed the pockmarks on Norinski's forehead disappear beneath angry wrinkles. The actor mumbled something, gave up the chase and said peevishly to Karás:

"You do write rubbish, my dear fellow. But I'll tell you this much, next time I'll play my Hamlet just like yesterday. It just so happens that I play *my* version. Do you understand, my boy?"

Karás swallowed something down and said something about the interpretation that other men had offered, important ones; he might only mention Kainz[4] or . . . The student Rezek emptied his glass fiercely, and Norinski said heatedly:

---

2. *Czas* (*Čas*) is the *Times*; *czay* (*čaj*), later in this sentence and throughout the story, is tea.

3. Bohush is an English transliteration of the Slavic Bohuš (Rilke used the German transliteration Bohusch), which is a short form of the names Bohuslav (God-praising) and Bohumil (God-loving).

4. Josef Kainz (1858–1910) was a well-known Austrian actor.

"My dear fellow, what does a German Hamlet matter to me? Surely you don't want to claim that we aren't allowed to have an opinion of our own? Is Shakespeare a German? Well then, what do the Germans matter to us? I draw my interpretation directly from the English, as it were."

"The only right way," sanctioned Pátek, stroking his fashionable pointed beard with manicured fingers.

"Besides, your costume, I mean from an artistic viewpoint . . . ," soothed the handsome painter, and Norinski promptly turned toward him. "Yes," he yawned with utter superficiality, and then went on in the condescending tone of a patron: "How is your play coming along, Machal?"

The lyric poet stared into his glass of absinthe for a while in silence and replied softly and plaintively, "It is spring."

They were all expecting something more, but the poet already seemed to be back on his way toward the pale garden of his dreams. He watched his absinthe glass grow larger and larger, until he felt himself in the very middle of the opal luminosity, very light, utterly dissolved in this unusual atmosphere. Only Schileder had taken the powerful utterance seriously. It lay upon him so thickly that he hesitated even to twitch his eyelids. Deep inside he thought: God, everyone brings that off. Has he said something special, then? I can do that too: It is . . . He couldn't finish it. Everyone was laughing, and Schileder began to breathe again as he saw from the expressions of the others that the utterance might not have been so weighty after all. Karás turned to the lyric poet: "That means your piece is flourishing, eh?"

Machal said to his muse with a bow, "Excuse me —," and came back reluctantly out of the opal world; but the misunderstanding was just too glaring. "No," he emphasized, "that means I am too depressed now. That means it's the time now when Nature misunderstands all growth, that means I am tired — tired of this sore budding."

"But, pardon me," the novelist tapped him on the shoulder with his fashionably yellow glove, "that may be so, but surely that isn't spring."

And the painter thought: No, that isn't spring.

" 'In the merry month of May,' " declaimed the actor.[5]

"Once," breathed the poet, making a motion with his hand as if to push this "once" even further back, "once it may have been like that, the way it says in old poems — spring: 'light and love and life.' Anyone who still believes that is lying to himself." He sighed deeply.

What a pity, thought the painter, so no more spring.

But Machal lifted his face, which was disfigured by large freckles, high into the clear afternoon light, and was barely able to see through the window the ramp of the National Theater, on which a policeman was pacing up and down. Now that was not particularly what he wanted to point out to anyone, but nevertheless he said:

"Just look outside. This fight against the stupid, un-ploughed clods, that each of the delicate, frail seeds must fight in order to reach its summer. Here," and he wriggled up a bit higher, "stands the helpless blossom wanting to bloom; that's the single thing she can do, she can only bloom, and she really doesn't want to disturb anyone, and yet they are all against her: the black topsoil, that lets her through only after lengthy pleading, the days that scatter warmth and rain and wind indiscriminately down on her, and the nights that creep up on her slowly in order to strangle her with their icy fingers. This cowardly, wretched fight, this is spring." Machal shivered; his eyes went dead. "King Bohush" stared at him with utter fixity. It was a very unjust thing that the poet was saying, it seemed to him, and he had much in his mind against it. He felt compelled to stand up and, towering and bright, defend the spring, which

5. This is the first line of a poem in Heinrich Heine's *Buch der Lieder* (*Book of Songs*), and the beginning of Robert Schumann's song cycle *A Poet's Love*, based on Heine's poetry; in other words, it is a well-known *German* quotation.

was still full of sun and success. So many beautiful thoughts rose to his head that his cheeks grew quite warm and he forgot, for a moment, to breathe. But, oh, what use would it have been to stand up; they would hardly have noticed, for Bohush almost looked taller sitting on the high velvet-covered bench than when he was standing. His voice, too, could hardly have flown far enough to reach Norinski; at such distances it already grew insecure and fluttered like a wounded bird. Bohush knew that. And so he remained silent; he pressed his lips, that might have been sculpted out of wood, close together and began, the way he often had as a child, to play quietly to himself with the many golden thoughts, building whole mountains and fortresses — and from the slender windows between their columns his dreams greeted him. He was so rich that he could erect new palaces each time, none of which resembled a former one; and that is saying something, for the little man had been pursuing this occupation for over thirty years, since the fifth year of his life perhaps — and yet he didn't have to repeat himself. The others were talking now (while Machal surely felt he was sitting back inside his glass of absinthe) about noisy matters and trivialities in incoherent confusion, and over it all the bass voice of the actor hovered with outspread wings. But Bohush, in his corner, composed his apology for Spring. Of course he actually knew Spring only as he appeared in the dark and damp Stag Moat[6] or in the Malvazinka graveyard[7]; once, as a child, he had seen him in the wild Sharka[8], and today he still heard within his breast a fine old

6. The Stag Moat (Hirschgraben or Jelení příkop) is a deep, natural moat on the northern side of Hradčany. It formed part of the castle's fortifications, and gained the name Stag Moat because it had been used by some of the Czech kings as a deer preserve.

7. A graveyard established in 1876 on property owned by Malvaz, a citizen of Prague, on the west bank of the Vltava. It is now a cemetery in the Smíchov district.

8. The Sharka (Šárka) is a deep valley on the western edge of Prague, through which the Šárka (a stream) flows into the Vltava.

echo of that sunny day. How blessed he must then be to look on out there where his homeland is, far from the city and its unrest, and it angered and pained Bohush that the people around him, who after all had been far afield, were allowing Spring to be renounced. Surely he had to tell them that. But a timid attempt of his lips succumbed quickly and without a trace to the general confusion, and poor Bohush wouldn't have known what more to say anyway. As if they feared betrayal, his thoughts fled in nervous turbulence out of the fine assembly, and in their place a single idea filled his brain, and he uttered it involuntarily and unnoticed: "Yes, my father." It took a moment before the hunchback realized why he was thinking of him just then. He saw him: in his enormous dark-blue braided coat with the collar that seemed to blend together with his great, full beard, he paced back and forth with broad, self-assured strides in the lofty, light-drenched entrance hall of the old ducal palace in Spurrier Street.[9] The golden knob on his staff nearly touched the golden fringe that hung from the brim of the three-cornered hat, beneath which his eyes were earnest and watchful. Then the small, sickly Bohush would often stand behind the door of the porter's lodge and gaze shyly through a slit at the powerful strides of his father, whose figure was taller than those of all the other men, so much more towering too than that of the aged duke, before whom his father doffed the braided hat very deeply without particularly bowing as he did so. As far back as his memory went, Bohush could not recall a kiss or a smile from this man, though certainly his figure and his voice were among the clearest impressions of his sorry childhood. And for this reason he would always think of his father at times when he envied the long-dead man those two attributes. He said to himself: Really, both

9. Spurrier Street is a translation of the German Spornergasse, which was originally the main road to Prague Castle and contains several significant baroque palaces. It is now called Nerudova ulice after the Czech writer Jan Neruda, who lived there.

are now as good as unused; he needs neither voice nor figure any more; why then did he take all that with him? And when the hunchback had these thoughts, the same thing always happened: all at once he felt something taking him along, tearing him away. His thoughts were no longer inside him, they ran ahead of him, and he had to pursue them in order to catch them again. Surely one couldn't just let them run loose like that. Breathless, he always overtook them at the same spot. It was a bright autumn night with flighty clouds. The fleeting light was just patient enough to allow Bohush to recognize a marble tablet, half hidden by wild branches, which read: Vítězslav Bohush, Porter to the Duke. And as often as the little man read this, he began to dig with greedy nails in the grass and the clods, until he became weaker and weaker and the damp earth's breath became heavier and steamier and his bloody nails finally scraped on the smooth wood of a large yellow coffin. And then he saw himself kneeling on the chest in the black pit and feeling at a loss for a second or two. Until the same solution always came to him: it must be possible to ram through this board with one's head, like a windowpane. Hadn't they always mocked him for the sake of his heavy skull? So it must be good for something, mustn't it? Crash! The board gives way — naturally — like a windowpane, and Bohush takes his father's breast with hot hands out of the dull darkness and buckles it like a harness around his shrinking shoulders, and he reaches in again and searches and searches with cramping fingers and sends the other hand in to help as well and can't understand at all that with both raw hands he can't find the voice of his father.

On the evenings of early spring there is a moist coolness to the air that lays itself softly over all colors and makes them lighter and more alike. The bright houses on the quay[10] have

---

10. The quay along which Bohush and Rezek are walking is the Smetana Quay (Smetanovo nábřezí) between the National Theater and Charles Bridge;

almost all taken on the pale hue of the sky; only their windows quiver now and again in hot gleams and, reconciled, die down in the dusk as soon as the sun no longer rouses them. Then only the tower of St. Vitus[11] stands there upright in its eternal hoary gray. "It is truly a landmark," said Bohush to the taciturn student. "It outlasts every twilight and is always exactly the same — I mean in its color. Don't you think so?"

Rezek hadn't heard a thing. He looked across to the bridge tower of the Lesser Town, where the lamps were just being lit.

Bohush continued: "I know my dear mother Prague to the heart — to the heart," he repeated, as if someone had questioned his claim, "because surely that is her heart, the Lesser Town with the Hradčany.[12] What is most secret is always in the heart, and you see, there are so many secret things in these old houses. I have to tell you this, Rezek, because you're from the country and you may not know it yet. But there are old chapels and, Jesus, what curious things they have there! Paintings and hanging lamps, and whole chests, Rezek, I'm not lying, whole chests full of gold. And passageways lead far out from these old chapels, far along under the whole city, maybe as far as Vienna."

Rezek looked at the hunchback from the side.

"By my soul," he swore, laying his hand on his crooked, stocky breast. "I wouldn't have believed it either. Never in my life. But I saw it once, not in a chapel, but . . ."

---

from there one sees a striking view of Hradčany and St. Vitus's Cathedral across the river.

11. St. Vitus's Cathedral forms part of Prague Castle on Hradčany. The Gothic building was begun in 1344; it is the mausoleum of the kings of Bohemia and houses the crown jewels.

12. The Hradčany or Castle Hill is the hill on the west bank of the Vltava that dominates the city, on which Prague Castle and St. Vitus's Cathedral are located. The Lesser Town (Malá Strana), originally a separate town dependent on the castle for its livelihood, was by Rilke's time an ultraconservative neighborhood lying between Hradčany and the river.

"Where?" the student probed suddenly, with such decided interest that the little man shrank back.

"You see," he said, "you won't believe it. But in our cellar, at the very end, there is a depression, about two steps down, and then a hole in the wall, just large enough for a person to crawl through — like this — on all fours of course." Bohush laughed his broken laugh.

"Well, then —," prompted Rezek, but added more softly, as he shaped a cigarette between fidgety fingers, "what of it?"

"I'd never have crawled in. God forbid. But one time the candle that I'd come downstairs with fell burning between old sticks of firewood. What a shock! Well, you can imagine, Rezek, a burning candle among old, dry wood. At last, I find it again; it had gone out, naturally, but in pure alarm I keep digging. There could have been a spark somewhere underneath, you know. Then suddenly I slide down deeper with the wood and I'm sitting in front of a hole. I look inside. Impossible. Another cellar, I think. I strike a light. But it's only a passageway, and it leads God knows how far, God knows."

They were now walking very slowly down the quay toward the stone bridge. Rezek took a long pull on his small, soggy cigarette and said, without looking down at Bohush: "Of course, it was bricked up long ago, that hole?"

"Bricked up?" giggled Bohush, "bricked up," and he could hardly get hold of himself in his merriment. "Who'd brick up something like that?"

"Well, you reported it in any case?" The student looked angry. His dark eyes lurked in his wan face as if to hurl themselves on the little man's reply.

That one had only just regained his composure. "You know, my mother — I told *her* about it. And she said, 'A hole? What does that have to do with us, Bohush. Pile the firewood back in front of it the way it was.' And so I piled the firewood in front of it, the way it was. She's right, after all — what does the hole have to do with us." The student nodded distractedly and then quickly said, "It still is cold in April." He pushed his angular shoulders higher and drew the shabby yellow summer coat, which he'd worn all winter, tightly together in front. "Shall we go over there into the café? A *czay* will do us good. Come on." He shoved his hand under the hunchback's arm and tried to pull him along. Bohush resisted. "What are you thinking of, Rezek? We were in the café long enough." "Well, yes, with *them*." The student laid a scornful stress on the last word. "I want to chat with *you*, Bohush; not with these great gentlemen, with these artists." "What are you saying," Bohush gasped, "the nation must be proud of them." Rezek stood still and grew very pale. "If only these people would be proud of the nation instead. But, believe me, they don't know a thing about each other — neither the nation about them, nor they about the nation. I ask you, what are they, are those Czechs, do you think? Just look at any one of them. That Karás writes in German newspapers about our art. And our art, what is that? Songs, perhaps, like the very young, healthy, barely awakened nation might sing? Stories of its strength and its courage and its freedom? Pictures of its homeland? Well? No trace of them! These gentlemen don't know a thing about it. They weren't born yesterday, like the nation, which is still utterly childlike, full of wishes and without a single fulfillment. They became mature overnight. Overripe. After all, that is so much more comfortable then the long, lonely way through oppression, the one the nation must travel, poor thing! That is almost effortless. One imports every-thing from Paris: clothes and convictions, thoughts and in-spiration. One was a child yesterday and today one is a young elder — surfeited. One suddenly knows it all. And after that one produces one's art. One paints scenes of horror and orgies. One looks for the whore in woman and glorifies her in novels; then one condemns this whore in frivolous songs and celebrates manly love in weighty strophes, and finally one has reached the goal: one no longer glorifies and one no longer condemns. One is tired of this. One is so far beyond it all. One is a mystic. One isn't even at home anymore here, in Bohemia; oh no, one has one's homeland somewhere — I don't know — at the primal fount of life. That *is* laughable, isn't it? While the nation stirs and for the first time feels how young and healthy it is and the new, timid strength of a beginning wells up in its veins, the artists profane its language by misusing its springtime for the sickly art of an ending." The student had talked himself hot and hoarse. They still stood in the same spot. Passersby began to take notice, and a policeman, too, sent a suspicious glance over from time to time. Bohush stared up at the student in silence, and he now seemed to him to loom just as tall and proud into the night as the ancient cathedral tower over there.

Now Rezek said in a changed voice, irritated by the people's curiosity, "Come on into the café then."

And Bohush, completely under the spell of this command, went along. He couldn't even imagine having said no. But when they paused at the door of the little café, he said timorously, "I really can't, Mr. Rezek, forgive me, but I really can't now. My mother, you know. She expects me in the evenings. And she'd worry if I didn't come. She's like that. Excuse me . . ."

The student interrupted him curtly. "Then I'll accompany you." He didn't even seem to feel cold any more now. And they went toward the Lesser Town. In silence. As they passed by the policeman, the hunchback sensed that Rezek caught a dark, suspicious glance from there. He looked up; but the student had already turned his head away and was spitting indifferently toward the other side, seemingly determined to hit the curb. Bohush considered; he sensed a kinship between the beautiful thoughts that had come to him that afternoon in the National and what Rezek had said and what he would still have to say. It was the first time that this sensation had come over him, although he often met with the student; he had always considered him a fool. Why? Perhaps because he usually kept silent? That was the reason they probably considered him, Bohush, to be of limited intelligence. On the other hand, though, how beautiful the student's face, which was in itself thin and ugly, had become during his enthusiastic speech. Everything in his face and his gestures that had looked angular and wooden received an accentuation into the sublime: it became stern, lordly, relentless. The whole of this young man who had shot up to such a height, who had grown too quickly, who was too poorly nourished and too wretchedly clothed, had quite unexpectedly taken on for Bohush something elemental, eternal, and as he walked along beside him like this, he couldn't rid himself of the feeling that he would have to make a point of remembering this day: Saturday, April 17. The notion grew very certain and clear in him, though seemingly in the background of his soul. At the front stood his own ego, which bowed and said to Bohush: I must decidedly refuse to tolerate that, most decidedly! You don't at all have the right, my dear fellow, to keep silent about all the treasures I give you, Bohush. Out with it. Speak. Let the people know that I'm rich. I know what you want to say. You are ugly. But just go ahead and speak. Speaking makes one beautiful. You've just had a chance to see it there. Promise me. And poor Bohush gave his ego his word of honor: Truly, from now on I will speak. And Bohush was about to begin, when the student stood still beside him and pointed across the Vltava and the forlorn lights that drifted on its high, dark waves. "Look at the Vyshehrad there, the old family seat of the Libusha,[13] and there the Hradčany, and behind us the

13. The Vyšehrad, located on the east bank of the Vltava toward the south of Prague, is the oldest Slavic castle. It was built in the ninth century by the legendary princess Libuše, who is said to have prophesied the founding of Prague.

Tyn Church, shrines, all of them.[14] If the gentlemen flee into the past, as they are always claiming, why not into this past? Why do they tell us of the Orient and the Crusades and the black Middle Ages? That's an artistic question, they say. No, I say: That is a question of the heart. It isn't coincidence that those distant things 'suit' them and the near, the familiar, has nothing to say to them. They are simply foreigners. And the nation anxiously tends its ancient, ungainly tradition, which despite all solicitude grows paler and paler from grandchild to grandchild, so that it hardly knows any more about the living riches of its homeland. Sure! It would, of course, be too degrading for these great gentlemen to accompany the people before their holy heirlooms and to tell them in new, clear words of their ancient worth and their dedicated dignity."

Bohush fixed his eyes on the stones in the pavement and, as if forcing himself, said softly, interrupted again and again by nervous coughing:

"You're right, Rezek, you are most certainly right. Of course I can't understand all this very well, because it's really not so simple, what you're saying here. But you are right. In fact, I've thought about this, sometimes. Why does one paint this and not that. Why does one write this way and not that way . . . but still, if you will allow me to say so, the fact that the poets don't tell stories about the Hradčany and the Tyn, that doesn't matter, that doesn't matter. I mean — look, I know my dear mother Prague to the heart, yes, and no poet ever told me anything about her. One only has to grow up in the midst of these churches and palaces. God knows they don't need anyone to speak for them, they speak themselves, I guess. If only one is willing to listen. Oh, what

14. The Týn Church, or Church of Our Lady of Týn, stands in Prague's Old Town Square (Altstadter Ring or Staroměstske náměstí). A Gothic building, founded in 1365, its two towers are a familiar part of the panorama of the city. At one time it was the principal Hussite church in Prague.

stories they know. My friend, I'd like to tell you a few of them sometime, all right? Or better yet: you ought to hear my mother talk about it."

Rezek made an impatient gesture. Bohush noticed it immediately and faltered a moment, then went on: "Pardon me. Actually the only other thing I wanted to say was . . . yes, so that about the Hradčany is nothing to feel sorry about, but the other thing is. That which isn't the past. The alleys here and these people and then especially the fields behind the city and the people there. Surely you've already seen it too: a field, you know, a sort of field without end, dreary and gray. And evening behind it. And nothing, only a few trees and a few people; the trees are bent over and the people too. Or a quarry, like the ones out there behind Smíchov.[15] From the gray, bald hill the little pieces of gravel roll down into the rubble basin. The sound of that! Yes, that too is a song; and down there men sit and pound the gray rocks all day long and make small, neat, smooth little cubes out of them and see a dull sun through the horn-rimmed glasses that they wear in front of their eyes. And the younger ones among them forget sometimes and begin to sing softly, no unruly song, God forbid, but one that suits the rhythm: 'Kde domov můj'[16] or something like that. And then all of them listen. It doesn't last long, though. It soon occurs to the youth that the gravel dust is too acidic, bad for the lungs, and so, well, he is quiet again . . . But you must pardon me . . ." The little man looked around helplessly, but got hold of himself again when he saw that the student's eyes were resting on him gravely and attentively. He took this as a sign of success, and with more assurance

15. Smíchov is the oldest western suburb of Prague. During the baroque period it contained upper-class villas, but these were replaced by factories, textile mills, and tenements during the nineteenth century, when it became known as an industrial slum inhabited by Czech workers.

16. "Where is my homeland," a song from the operetta *Fidlovačka* (1834) by Czech dramatist J. K. Tyl, set to music by F. J. Škroup. Since 1918 it has been the Czech national anthem.

than before went on with his speech: "The only other thing I wanted to say was: Why don't they paint this, why? Why don't they compose something like this? Surely this is Czech — it is so sad."

Rezek only nodded and said, "Do you think the nation is very sad?"

Bohush reflected. "Of course," he then said hesitatingly, "actually I know so little; I never get around very much. But I do think so."

"Why?"

"Why, you ask? God, do I know? The parents are sad, and the children are too and they stay that way. When they can barely walk, they see the gloomy Nepomuk[17] in front of the door holding the Crucified One in his arms, and the old willow by the village pond, and the sunflowers in the little garden, which tire so early in the still sun. Does that make one happy? And then they learn hate so early. The Germans are everywhere, and one has to hate the Germans. I ask you, what for? Hate makes one so sad. Let the Germans do what they like. They don't understand our country, and because of that they can't ever take it away from us. At the borders, no doubt, there are large forests and highlands where the Germans are very firmly established, aren't there? But they really only frame the country. What lies in between, the many fields and meadows and streams, that is our homeland, that belongs to us, as we belong to it with all that is in us."

"As slaves," Rezek threw in contemptuously.

"Don't say that. Please. Not as slaves. As children. Maybe not as fully legitimate children, not fully entitled to their inheritance — for the moment. But still as true, natural

---

17. St. John of Nepomuk, general vicar of the archbishops of Prague, was thrown into the Vltava River from Charles Bridge in 1393 on the orders of King Wenceslas IV. He was canonized in 1729. In 1681 a memorial to him was erected on Charles Bridge, the oldest of the statues of saints that line the bridge.

children. You must feel it. You say yourself: the nation is very young and healthy; then it will certainly also be strong and will not give in. It's possible that one or another of us bears chains — for today. That will pass. I know that someone has written 'Songs of a Slave,' one of the older generation.[18] He's wrong. No honest man of our nation makes noise with his chains. Certainly not. He even lifts them up carefully when he walks, so that the dear earth will not notice anything of his distress . . . That's how the upright among us are."

Now they had just reached the beginning of Bridge Street[19]; they passed through the denser crowds of pedestrians and turned quickly into the first narrow side street. In the glow of the next lantern the student surveyed his companion with undisguised astonishment. He shook his head, seemed to quash something on his lips and said, "You are an orator, Bohush."

"Oh," the little man let out, looking utterly gratified.

"No, seriously. But, let me tell you, that part about the Germans . . . If you are sensible, perhaps the nation will have need of you someday."

"Whaaat?" Bohush let out, almost laughing with shock and distraction. But Rezek had pressed his lips firmly together; he looked very solemn and said nothing. The hunchback became quite alarmed. He pressed closer to the student and whispered:

"I just think all of this to myself. Really. Of course I don't know. Maybe it's really all different. I really can't say very well. You mustn't think badly of me, Mr. Rezek." And suddenly he became utterly discouraged. "You see, I'm really such a poor fellow. If you only knew how poor I am; in the

18. An allusion to *Písně otroka* (1895) by the patriotic writer Svatopluk Čech (1846–1908).
19. Bridge Street (Brückengasse or Mostecká ulice) leads from Charles Bridge to the Lesser Town Square. The real-life "Bohush," Rudolf Mrva, lived at 13 Bridge Street with his mother (see Introduction).

morning I'm a copyist in the editorial office, and in the evening, then I'm with my mother; she's so old and she can hardly see anymore. It's like that every day. And Sundays, when I see my Frantishka, do you know where we spend our time? In the Malvazinka. There where the green crosses stand, each one exactly like the others. Only children lie there, and on the narrow metal plates there's always only some Christian name, 'little Karel' or 'little Marie,' and a prayer along with it. That's how it is there. And there we spend our time on Sundays. 'Here we are alone, *milatshku*,'[20] says my Frantishka. 'Yes,' I say, 'Frantishka, here we are alone.' And all along I know that we're among all the dead. Does that matter? There's still something in between, sometimes spring, sometimes snow. Oh, I'm really such a poor fellow."

"Now, now," Rezek consoled him, and already they were standing in front of the house in which Bohush shared two rooms under the roof with his elderly mother. The student seemed to be in a hurry. "So you're not angry with me, Mr. Rezek," the hunchback pleaded. "There's no reason for that," the other said quickly, "now good night. No doubt I'll see you tomorrow at the café!"

"Yes, tomorrow, maybe — although it is Sunday, so I'll have to go with my Frantishka — yes — good night."

Rezek, who had already taken a few steps, suddenly turned back. He laid his unquiet hand on the little man's shoulder and added very quickly, with no particular emphasis:

"Honestly, you've made me curious, Bohush, you really have. Wouldn't you lead me into the cellar sometime . . . ?"

"Cellar?"

"Oh, you know, to that hole."

"Oh, yes, if you like, of course."

"Good, then let's make it soon — when?"

20. *Miláčku*, beloved.

"Whenever you like."

"Tomorrow morning?"

"Tomorrow morning."

And they fixed the hour.

No one noticed that early on Sunday Bohush led a guest into the cellar of the old, dark house in Hieronymus Street. The two had, after all, descended as carefully as if they were trying not to wake someone who was asleep; they had moved the firewood away at the bottom, and then the stranger, who spoke very little, had taken the lantern and crawled into the secret passage. The hunchback stood and stared after him. For a while the hole remained lit; then the rays of light went out there at the edges, and then a few reflections fluttered back and forth in the black frame, pounded their wings raw on the stone walls and fell dead in the boundless darkness. Bohush listened. Steps echoed far and still farther away. All at once fear overcame him. Why is he doing this? he thought. At last he no longer heard any steps, and now he began to call out. His words had a peculiar sound: they carried with them the pounding of his heart, which he felt in his throat and which grew steadily wilder and more tumultuous. "Be careful, Rezek! Rezek, don't go any further. What are you doing? Now, now! You mustn't go any further. Here, here! Do you hear? Jesus Mary, where are you? No fooling around, one never knows . . ." Suddenly the full light of the lantern fell on him; it came so unexpectedly that the little man retained, for a while, all the signs of terror and fright and looked comical enough in his breathless confusion. Rezek was beside him with a single leap, but didn't seem to notice him at all. A certain satisfaction gleamed up in his dark eyes, then quickly went out, and that stern taciturnity came over his face that turned every line in it to stone. "Well?" Bohush finally managed, taking the lantern out of the other's hand in order to have the light very close by and very safe. The student suddenly seemed to him rather simple, almost a bit queer, and when he noticed, too, that in his fright he had spent the whole time calling toward the opposite side, where there was no hole at all, his constriction melted and seemed to flow from his body in unruly, tinny laughter. Now he was in a mood to find everything funny, and it seemed to him a precious joke that the haggard student was piling the firewood back up in front of the secret door and treating the task with such significance and solemnity. While ascending the steps he invited Rezek to come up to his place this time after all. No doubt his mother would still be at home too, and he wouldn't regret hearing fine stories and maybe also drinking a little glass of *gilka*[21] (yes, even he, poor Bohush, possessed such delicacies). The student excused himself curtly. He had urgent commitments and would come another time. It had, incidentally, been very interesting down there — and he owed many thanks. Bohush was very disappointed; he would so have liked to tell stories now. But Rezek couldn't be persuaded. He said a hasty good-bye and departed, hearing the hunchback, waddling overeagerly up the stairs, call a very loud "good morning" to someone or other on the first floor. The student walked hurriedly up Bridge Street. He made the impression that a terribly busy man makes among idlers, and his slim, black figure seemed to help itself along by means of the light and lingering Sunday strollers who were streaming toward the Church of St. Nicholas.[22]

Among the festive crowd the wretched figure of "King Bohush" surfaced not much later. In this neighborhood most people knew him, knew the derisive nickname that he, God knows why, had borne since his schooldays, and presumptuous boys probably hurled a snickering "King Bo-

21. A caraway-flavored liquor.
22. St. Nicholas's Church in the Lesser Town Square (Kleinseitner Ring or Malostranské náměstí) is the largest and most magnificent high-baroque building in Prague, built between 1704 and 1755. After 1773, it became the main parish church of the Lesser Town.

hush" at his back, which was much rounder and uglier still under the black Sunday suit. The hunchback didn't let this bother him. He followed with the crowd a while, but then turned around and walked, still smiling, toward the Old Town.[23] He wanted to encounter someone; he felt disposed to explain to someone or other that life, while it may have its sharp edges, is nevertheless on the whole quite an excellent thing, that the Czechs are a patriotic and a magnificent nation and Prague a city — ("please, just have a look at this Rudolphinum,"[24] he would have said now) — a city, the like of which was not to be seen anywhere around. The possibility of finding someone was greatest in Ferdinand Street and on the "Moat,"[25] on the broad sidewalks of which all of modern Prague spends Sunday noon, and he steered toward there in the hope of seeing this or that one — even if it were Machal or Pátek. The thought had hardly crossed his mind when he recognized Pátek. The elegant novelist was strutting along just in front of him. He was wearing a brand new light-gray suit with which he patronized, as it were, the somewhat timid spring, and the sharp pleats remained unbroken while he walked and reached faultlessly down to the gleaming patent-leather shoes, which he knew how to show off gracefully. When Bohush, who had over-

23. The Old Town, located on the east bank of the Vltava, is one of the originally independent cities that joined together to form Prague; the others are Hradčany, the Lesser Town, and the New Town.

24. The Rudolphinum, or House of Artists, in Jan Palach Square is a neo-Renaissance building built between 1876 and 1884. Originally a concert hall and art gallery, it served as the Parliament building during the First Republic. It is now called the Dvořák Concert Hall and is home to the Czech Philharmonic Orchestra and the Academy of Music.

25. The promenades of Prague at the turn of the century. Beginning at the National Theater on the bank of the river, Ferdinand Street (now Národní třída or National Street) runs as far as St. Wenceslas Square (Wenzelsplatz or Václavské náměstí), where it is continued by the "Moat" ("am Graben" or Na příkopě) as far as the Powder Tower. Both streets are built on top of the original fortifications of the Old Town; avenues of linden trees grew up along the filled-in moat during the late eighteenth century.

taken him, addressed him, he laid a gloved hand (*café au lait*, 6¾) casually on the brim of his short top hat and showed little inclination to enter into a conversation. But Bohush was so happy to have found someone that he forgot his shyness and simply went along without waiting for any encouragement. Now and then Pátek did throw down some word or other — that is to say, he let it drop, paying scant attention to whether the little man caught up these precious fragments or not. The latter, in contrast, talked incessantly and reposed now and again in his loud laughter. Everything provided him with material. His jokes, which were not always very fortunate, aroused attention or annoyance right and left, and the fashionable young man, who was imparting greetings in all directions, felt thoroughly uncomfortable in the company of this "unfortunate proletarian," as he was in the habit of calling Bohush. At the next corner he acted as if he recognized a good friend on the other side of the street; he peered across for a while, mumbled something indistinctly and, before Bohush grasped what was going on, skipped away. The hunchback went on; after ten steps he paused once again, looked for the figure of the escapee in the crowd opposite, and realized that Pátek was walking alone. The laughter faded from his broad face; he hurled an angry word at someone who had brushed against him in passing, not even very roughly; then he turned around and thrust his way with ruthless shoulders through to a side street, where there was no sun and not a soul. He had tears in his eyes.

For a while he thought of looking up Schileder in his studio. He was always tolerated there. Even if the painter happened to be busy, he was allowed to crawl into a cosy corner of the large room with some portfolio or other and could contemplate pictures for hours and let his eyes run along the high shelves on the wall, where the most incongruous things, the most eccentric gadgets, stood and kept each other company behind the thick veils of year-old dust. He had often sat there unnoticed hour after hour, and when he could discover somewhere a piece of velvet or a colorful silk with gleaming folds he wouldn't let the cloth out of his sight again, and the painter would willingly make him a present of it. Then he'd always stormed hastily up his four flights of stairs, wild with impatience to put on the piece of stuff and step in front of the mirror. Yes, poor Bohush regarded his black suit, which was too old in any case, as a very wretched, unworthy Sunday dress; even as a child he'd dreamed of being able to go out among people in extraordinary and magnificent clothes. He had also, for the sole purpose of obtaining the red choir robe, ministered at high mass during his school days, and, for the sake of the gleaming uniform alone, he would later have liked nothing more than to turn soldier. That was all long past, and now he could no longer hope ever to put on anything else, even for the greatest festivity, than this black, shabby suit — except if Frantishka should yet decide to marry him. For this celebration he would not hesitate to have a new one made, and then it would have to have a wide velvet collar. His father's embroidered vest awaited this day as well, and Bohush would then have it tailored to fit — only when the time was at hand. Just don't spend the money for nothing. And would the time ever be at hand? . . . Last Sunday Bohush had waited in vain for his beloved. What if she stayed away again today?

This is how it is in the poorer graveyards, where no mighty marble gravestones are ornamented with calculating artistry by a gardener's hand: Spring, in his innocence, enters, and the rattling of the rusty iron gate is the last noise he hears. He has no idea where he is. But he must like it within these still walls, with life surging far away behind them, and among these gleaming little ceramic angels who have folded their hands to pray to him. To whom else? Besides, there is no better prop for the young, timid winds than a cross like this, on which they, once they have ventured so high, can stretch out as far as they like to the right or the left, as if for a reward. And because he is so well off, Spring grows up sooner in a place like this than anywhere else. The small, dark figure of Bohush at least was plainly lost in the bustle of primroses and anemones, and above him the wind lurked in a tree that bore blossoms before the leaves had come out, and now and then the wind sent a blossom into his lap and rocked the dainty branches roguishly, as if in the next second he intended to bury the solitary visitor in piles upon piles. But the hunchback was in no mood to understand him. He dusted the blossoms sullenly from his black sleeves and looked past the sunny Sunday into a different, a very different day. That was in a graveyard, too. About three years ago. A few people, dressed in black, stood around the open grave. The men in a certain cavalierlike elegance with their great beards or completely clean-shaven faces and those folds around the lips which, by common consent, are signs of mourning and deep emotion; the women, much more inconsequential, with handkerchiefs in their hands; and, at the midpoint of this solemn group, a small, helpless, white-haired woman. She was completely overwhelmed by her pain; it possessed her totally. Each twitch of her poor figure, each plea of her choked voice belonged to it. Because of this she had forgotten everything around her, even her son, poor Bohush. He was utterly astonished. He had never seen his mother like this. He himself didn't feel at all out of the ordinary. He was simply thinking about how his father could ever have found enough room in the coffin. The casket hadn't looked overly large, and he'd probably have to lie like *this*. And he pictured to himself how his father had drawn up his knees a little, and reflected that if the dead man ever had the admittedly quite unheard-of idea of stretching his legs, the yellow box would most certainly give way, either at the bottom or at the top. Filled with such meditations, he waited quietly for the company to take up the return journey. But when even now his incessantly weeping mother refused to recognize him in her pain, he became quite alarmed. He couldn't understand that the poor little woman, through all the forty years of her marriage, the first two perhaps excepted, had never dared to cry for fear of her husband, who would not tolerate a scene, and that she was now unconsciously enjoying the relief of a sort of liberation, crying away all that she had missed, one year after the other. And forty years can't be cried away at the flick of a wrist. Bohush looked in perplexity from one to the other. They all passed by him, the friends and companions of the deceased, and the most tactful among them pressed his hand in silence, while each time the eyes of the accompanying woman overflowed; and the royal valet said in a foreigner's precise High German: "He wasn't very old yet, your father." Whereby he meant to emphasize that the deceased had been two years older than he himself, His Serene Highness's English valet. Bohush became more anxious with each handshake; it only now occurred to him that something extraordinary must have happened after all. Fearing the stiff ceremoniousness of these people, he lagged several steps behind the train. Then suddenly he felt two arms descend toward him, and as he looked up, a young blonde female had just kissed him on the forehead. She had cool lips, he felt that, and what pleased him even more was that she wasn't crying. She only had very, very sad eyes. But when the hunchback met her gaze, he thought of a dark forest. Not of anything dreadful, just of a dark forest, in which one might very well make one's home. So the sad eyes were at once dear to him, the sad eyes of his Frantishka.

Incidentally, no one knew the woman then, no one in the entire funeral party knew her name; she had simply come along. At the gate of the graveyard stood two old beggar women, rosaries between their withered fingers. They were on the seventeenth Hail Mary. When Bohush, hand in hand with his new friend, passed by, they interrupted their prayer, and one of them said with a smirk, "That one there with the hunchback, that was the darling of the dear departed." And their hissing sniggers gradually became the eighteenth Hail Mary. But Bohush hadn't heard.

He saw the blonde girl again, and once when she caressed his forehead with her hand and said, "You are such a good, good, fellow," he kissed that hand, his heart beating rapidly. He had felt something run cold as ice down his back and everything thunder together in his head, had pressed his hands into one another so hard that he wanted to cry out in pain; then, instead of crying out, he had whispered, "You are my darling, aren't you?" And then she had laughed, laughed loudly and nodded, and her eyes were full of the dear sadness. But that was already long ago, and Bohush, sitting now under the blossoming tree in the Malvazinka, would so have liked to ask Frantishka about it again. Instead he gazed fixedly into the red face of the evening and knew: she won't come any more. There wasn't even the slightest hope in him; nevertheless, he remained seated between the mounds and crosses, spellbound by the dark wish to be allowed to dwell here with exactly the same right as his many neighbors. What would it require? Oh God, his eyes had simply to let go of those towers over there, those roofs, this softly melting slope, they would have to take leave of the sky, of the first evening star, and something deep inside him would have to draw one last breath and say "Frantishka," and then no more. That would be all, and is that so hard?

It must be hard after all, for Bohush got up and walked down the trickling driveway through to the broad main street. A gray, glimmering fog seeped downward there and held the gas flames as if suspended in air, so that they couldn't scatter any of their light down onto the dense crowds of tired excursionists who, ghostlike, took shape out of the infinite only two steps in front of the solitary figure and directly behind him sank back into the void. And if Bohush, following his innermost instinct, had walked on without looking up, he would surely have ended up in the

Vltava, which was still furious with breaking ice, the way a tired nag finds its way into the still stall — without looking up. But Bohush *looked up.* The mists around him began to speak to him in powerful, swelling tones, and all the towers from which he had recently wanted to take leave lifted up their solemn Ave-voices. It was as if some great festival were being celebrated up above the roofs, behind the impenetrable damp folds, and the hunchback's soul was suddenly up there, and before he could prevent it, it rose in the mystical jubilation of the breezes. And poor Bohush stood and gazed after it.

He remembered that in a week it would be Easter Sunday, and that filled him with so much joy that he came in to his elderly mother with a smile and had such amusing things to relate all evening long that the old woman became weak and dizzy from all the laughter. What did it matter that Bohush later dreamed that he and Frantishka were getting married? He saw it all exactly down to the very smallest details, down to the garnet earrings that hung like drops of blood from his bride's earlobes. And everything went according to plan. The wedding was in the great domed church of St. Nicholas, and Bohush even recognized the priest at once. Up to that point things went along sensibly, as in the light of day. But all at once it grew quite strange. A young, oh, such a young girl threw her arms around the bride, who was kneeling before the altar at his side, and cried, "I won't let you have him, I love him so!" She cried this very loudly, very wildly — although they were, if you please, in the great and solemn church of St. Nicholas. It was only natural that the bridegroom (he really wore, by the way, a new suit with a dark-red velvet collar) wanted to take a closer look at this very young girl who loved him so. He recognized Carla, Frantishka's younger sister, whom he knew only slightly, and he was very annoyed at this interruption. But when he did look more carefully, he perceived that this blonde child was wearing a nun's habit and — he was so abruptly surprised by joy, that he started and awoke. It was a while before, sitting up in bed, he came to himself. Then he calculated how long it was until Maundy Thursday; and when only three days appeared in between, Bohush smiled and, with this smile, slept dreamlessly into the morning.

In spite of the pitiful avenue that crosses it, the square in front of the royal castle in Prague looks quite grand. This is because it is completely framed by palaces. Most imposing is the broad brow of the old royal castle with the large white forecourt, behind the baroque railings of which the untiring watchman oscillates back and forth.[26] The family seat of the Prince of Schwarzenberg[27] and another, rather tedious building look on as if caught in an eternal obeisance, and to the right of the castle the newly painted palace of the archbishop keeps watch, in a rather ostentatious pose, over the small residences of the prelates and canons, which fawn close around their mighty patron.[28] At one corner only, to the side of the castle, where the Town Hall Steps[29] and the steep Spurrier Street open out, a gap has remained, and deep within, in glorious panoramas, squeezed between Lawrence Mountain and the Belvedere,[30] lies Prague — that rich, enor-

26. The main entrance to Prague Castle is through the First Courtyard, the newest of the castle's three courtyards. It was built in the 1760s, when the moats to the west of the castle were filled in and a baroque courtyard was constructed, along with an imposing grille separating the courtyard from Hradčany Square.

27. Built between 1545 and 1563 as the Lobkowitz Palace, this imposing Renaissance building came into the possession of the Schwarzenbergs in 1719. It now houses a military museum.

28. The Archbishop's Palace, dating from the sixteenth century, was restyled several times before being given its present rococo appearance in 1763 and 1764.

29. The Town Hall Steps (Schloßstiege or Radnické schody) connect the upper end of Nerudova ulice (here, Spurrier Street) with Hradčany Square.

30. Lawrence Mountain is a translation of Rilke's German Laurenziberg (Petřín), a hill to the south of Hradčany that is covered with gardens and parkland. The Belvedere, or Royal Summer Palace, is a small Renaissance palace,

mous epic of architecture. Full of light and life it spreads itself out before the eyes of Hradčany, and worthy new, shining stanzas are always joining themselves to its ancient ones. At the other end of the row of houses that appears bounded on one side by this lucid lookout lies an ancient, mean, one-story building, which stands there day in, day out, with its hands in front of its eyes, unwilling to behold any of the nearby splendor.[31] Children from all the surrounding area pass its solemn silence with shy shivers, and if they ever have stories told them about this house, then they probably can't sleep the whole night, or else they have fervid dreams, in which pale nuns do strange deeds. No doubt that *would* give wings to the young imagination, to hear that the Barnabite sisters, who forever live their mute dying within these gruesome walls, never exchange a word even among themselves, and are not even permitted to grant each other so much sun as one of them can find in the eyes of another; that they must survive their nights, torn by fearful prayers, in the wooden coffins in which they are finally — it would probably not be very long — laid in the plot of earth that was supposed to be in the very center of the dark walls and to which spring surely never found its way. The brother order of these Barnabite penitents has long since died out. The half-disintegrated skulls of its last two members lie on a stone altar in the forgotten catacomb vaults of Our Lady Victorious,[32] enjoying the prayerless quiet of

the summer residence of Queen Anna, in the Royal Garden north of Hradčany. It dates from 1538 to 1563 and is considered an outstanding example of Italian Renaissance architecture.

31. The Church of St. Benedict on Hradčany was given to the Barnabite order by Emperor Ferdinand II in 1627 and expanded into a monastery, which was inhabited by the Barnabites until 1786. In 1792, the empty building was donated by Emperor Leopold II to the Carmelite sisters. Although Rilke knew the history of the building, he follows the custom of Prague natives in referring to the inhabitants of the convent (incorrectly) as Barnabites. His description of the nuns, however, characterizes them as Carmelites.

32. The earliest baroque church in Prague, located at the base of Petřín. It

decay. But the sisters are much more tenacious in their suffering. When, fifteen years ago, the rusty remains of the doornails were disturbed for the last time, white-haired people from the neighborhood, and pious biddies with dubiously reliable memories, claimed that to the seven still-living sisters an eighth had been added — but those were really rather groundless suppositions. To be sure, however, younger and more keen-eyed individuals had also looked inside the carriage that was bringing the new victim, and these swore that it had been a very young girl of indescribable loveliness and refinement, and they said it was a sin to allow this wealth of rare charm to wither away in the most dreadful of all cloisters. And they had more to say, but much of it was gossip about the reasons which might have called forth this early leave-taking from life. Great romantic stories were constructed, all manner of daggers flashed in all manner of Bengali fires, and the most demonic princes of all fairyland drew their potential for existence from these suppositions. Of course, it was known for certain that some crass and fearsome deed lay behind this renunciation, and it was, as always, forgotten that it could perhaps have been some very quiet suffering, one of those deep, soundless disappointments that give to the most delicate souls the darkly known conviction that the peaks and valleys of experience are past, and that now the wide, wide plain with small ditches and ridiculous hillocks will begin, through which it is so tiring to wander. The lovely, tired child came out of the high, dark, ducal residence in Spurrier Street in which Bohush too used to play his shy boyish games, and the day on which the closed carriage brought the Princess Aglaya to her new, lonely home represented for him, too, who was at the time half-grown, a cutoff point. Actually he couldn't

---

was built by German Lutherans in 1611 to 1613, but since 1624 it has belonged to the Order of the Barefoot Carmelites.

even picture to himself what the princess looked like at that time; he bore inside him her image from the days when her golden laughter fluttered like an erring swallow through the solemn halls, and finally, in defiance of the stiff and shocked Englishwoman, lost itself in the free latitudes of the rustling park. There the two children met one another quite often and chattered and joked and chased one another, the way children will do who have rid themselves of a restraint: Aglaya of her governess and Bohush of his still, loyal sadness. Then years followed in which the porter's son didn't see his playmate, who had meanwhile become a lady, and so it happened that in his remembrances he pushed the day of her renunciation hard up against those hours of jubilant childhood, and it felt to him as if the most shining day were at once transformed into the very deepest night, the richest summer into the most desolate winter day — without a transition. He stood before an event the ruthlessness of which shocked him and the significance of which was apt to take from him forever the opinion that the rich and the privileged are, as it were, the allies of destiny, which confronts only the poor devil with enmity and hatred. At that time a whole bundle of prejudices fell all at once out of his hands; something of a worldview, of a religion was granted him, seeds that might have matured in him and perhaps also outward from him, if he had been bolder. But what might have become deeds that grow freely and festively out of a strong body became strange, colorful dreams in the wretched hunchback, shy raptures that touched an ever smaller world and at last formed only a thin halo around the princess's picture. His helpless gratitude ornamented this picture for so long that the laughing, loving child became a pale, secret beloved and the beloved a revered saint, who closely resembled the Virgin Mary and who would become utterly absorbed in listening to the extraordinary wishes of Bohush, and in accepting patiently all the splendid attributes that his untiring fantasy ascribed to her. And what an advantage

Bohush had over all other believers through this, that his saint, if beyond the reach of all the world, nevertheless lived and knew of him as of a confidant of her childhood — something she must have taken with her as a single jewel inside the eternal walls. This relationship did not suffer the least disturbance when the hunchback called Frantishka his beloved, for by that time the apotheosis of Aglaya was already so far advanced that her rarefied figure stood high above all petty desires and sultry dreams. Bohush dedicated himself to her only once a year — that is, on Maundy Thursday, the day on which the convent church of the Barnabites stands open to every visitor. This small, dark, and rather unadorned church is completely sealed off by a wall behind the main altar, on the other side of which the sisters of the order participate in the public mass. On the day before the Christian Good Friday — and on this day only — the nuns' voices trickle very quietly through the wall of the altar and sink like a distant lamentation onto the few worshippers. Then the small congregation strains its ears, holds its breath anxiously, and shivers, the priest at the altar interrupts his prayers, the altar boys glance fearfully into the black corners of the room, and the dark images on the walls awaken. Then the altar boy's clear bell breaks the spell. The images on the walls are dead once again, the priest bends over the chalice, and the pious shift in their pews, blow their noses loudly and whisper, "It was so faint; are there really still eight?" — and then one shrugs and sighs and blows one's nose.

So it was on this Maundy Thursday as well. Bohush knelt at the very front and waited for his saint to call. He had not forgotten the sound of her voice and always believed with complete conviction that he recognized her singing in the distant choral song. He caught it up and disengaged it from the whole like a silk thread out of a faded tapestry. He seemed to forestall it and allow only the rest to reach the other listeners. But today he knew at the first note: she was missing. And no matter how his terror tried to deny it, he knew: she was missing. And he leaned far forward, and his fear scouted out and throttled every tiniest sound, but he became ever more certain: she was missing. Finally, in boundless anxiety he stretched out his hands, far, far out — and listened with all his fingertips . . . she was missing. And then something in him cried out together with the altar boy's bell, a single time it cried out, and then he broke down on the hard pew like one whose god has forsaken him.

The painter Schileder was the first to notice a great change in Bohush. He reflected briefly on its possible causes, but remained completely in the dark. His wife Mathilde couldn't be of any help either. So they forgot about the astonishing circumstance until one morning, shortly after Easter Sunday, when Pátek entered the studio and said: "What insolence." Schileder laid down brush and palette and regarded the agitated man, who, without having taken off his hat, was pacing up and down: "Good morning, what's the matter with you?" But the novelist merely said a few more times, "What insolence," then stood still and tried very gingerly to set down the impeccable top hat on a stack of dusty portfolios. First he touched it lightly with his gloved fore-finger and pulled back as if he had touched a red-hot oven. With moving helplessness, he balanced the hat back and forth between the palms of his hands and threw the painter a reproachful glance. "Everything here is full of dust," he hesitated, "one can't even put anything down." At last he felt himself secure, sat down, and then related in considerable confusion how he'd come out of the National, they'd all been together there and discussed all sorts of things. "Don't you have a cigarette?" he interrupted himself, and continued only after Schileder had satisfied his demand. So they'd talked about all sorts of things. And that one — well, the "unfortunate proletarian" — had taken part in the debates in such a conspicuous and aggressive manner that he, Pátek, finally felt it his duty to teach this brash individual a lesson once and for all. "Don't you have any cognac?" he asked at this gripping moment. He tossed back the cognac and said with a grimace, while he raised himself up with his arms and stepped to the window, "And do you know what that fellow dares to do? He contradicts me. Have you ever heard anything like that, he contradicts me. Not only that, he insults me. He has the nerve to insult me." "Why, what did he say?" inquired the painter. "I don't know." Schileder looked at him with astonishment, so that he added quickly, not without embarrassment: "Well, do you think I have time to remember such nonsense; that I was ashamed to be seen with him, or something like that. The point is — just imagine: he insults me. How can one not be ashamed of that fellow!" For a moment more the elegant novelist seemed severely indignant, but he was already conceiving an interest in Schileder's work; he regarded this and that; carefully, between thumb and forefinger, he lifted up various frames that were standing there facing the wall. Schileder tolerated this good-naturedly, and wasn't surprised either when the young man soon took leave of him in the sunniest of moods. Pátek did this all the time. In a brief, more or less effective scene he came to terms with an annoying circumstance, finished with it once and for all, "overcame it," as he was in the habit of expressing himself. That didn't stop the great Overcomer from telling the Bohush story five more times that same morning, indeed in a more and more advantageous light, so that the fifth version, which was left in a modern operetta singer's boudoir, involved the charming representation of a dualistic philosophy of life, the good principle of which was victoriously embodied in the stylish figure of the narrator.

And the thing that everyone, in part through personal experience, in part through Pátek's disseminations, finally knew, did have a kernel of truth: Bohush had become a different person. His beloved and his saint had abandoned him. Thus he became aware that he had given these two figures so much of himself that now only a very small remnant remained his own. He wrestled for a few more hours over whether he should toss this last asset untouched into the Vltava or whether his capital was still substantial enough to be profitably invested in the great bank of life. In the course of this reflection a sentence suddenly occurred to him that settled the matter. Rezek had said to him on that memorable evening, "Perhaps the nation will have need of you someday." Of course, Rezek had also said, "If you are sensible." And that he was now more sensible than ever before, on that Bohush was willing to take an oath. He was bolder, too. He thought about many things and expressed what he thought, wherever it could be done, in somewhat old-fashioned, long-winded sentences, and he was on these occasions his own most attentive listener. Only very seldom, as if out of forgetfulness, did he grow shy and reticent; he himself dreaded these moments, in which the old Bohush with his silent, golden thoughts stood before him like a specter and implored him to return to the still sadness of the former days. But Bohush remained steadfast. All day long he was in the café and on the street, he sang, whistled and laughed, so that people turned around to look at him, he stood in front of the store windows staring at nothing else but the restless reflection of his own ugliness, and he was as one who expected something that doesn't happen every day. Almost by instinct he sought, above all, to encounter Rezek. He felt he had to hear it from *his* mouth, what *the* event for him would be. Only he couldn't get hold of the student anywhere. The latter had moved out of his apartment without leaving an address, and in the National no one professed to have seen him. "He's a peculiar fellow," Norinski said once. Schileder nodded, but the new Bohush scoffed, "He's a fool," and laughed his old, pitiful laugh, with which no one joined in.

On the evening of that day the strange event took place. Bohush, who was also neglecting his elderly mother more and more, came home later than usual. Holding aloft a burning match, he took a few steps upstairs. His gaze penetrated the dense darkness of the narrow, crooked hallway. It seemed to him as if the cellar door were not completely closed; he felt his way over there, tried it, opened it cautiously, and glided with rare decisiveness down the familiar cellar steps. His figure dissolved completely in the damp darkness, out of which distant, unfamiliar noises struck his ear. He kept on feeling his way noiselessly along the cold wall, and only when he found the firewood pushed to one side and noticed that a timid glimmer of light was coming toward him out of the secret passage did he feel fear. But another, more powerful emotion forced him closer. First he listened to the voices next door, and when he couldn't understand anything, he pushed himself with an involuntary movement, the skillfulness of which surprised him, just far enough into the opening so that he filled the doorframe, without projecting into the space beyond. What he recognized next was, not far in front of him on the ground, a large lantern, which poured out an intense light that floated on the flagstones like a thin, spilled liquid. Around the borders of this pool of light young male feet and right in the middle of the circle the feet of a young girl. His gaze fastened on these, crept slowly upward along a dress of uncertain color and found, in the semi-darkness, two bright, lively, girlish hands, which were bringing impassioned gestures to the aid of the words that Bohush still could not understand. But he understood the hands. He suddenly grasped that these wild hands were shaking something, that they sought to topple some injustice with their young and holy turbulence. And he began to love these hands. Gently he raised his head and sought the face to go with these beloved hands. His eye fought a brief, stubborn battle with the envious shadows, which were constantly blurring the barely discovered features, until it finally triumphed. He recognized Carla. And now he waited expectantly, and his amazed and wondering gaze, in defiance of the darkness, never again left the lovely, enthusiastic visage of the young girl. He sucked the words from her lips until they took on a personal tone for him, and that was the one out of the dream: "I love him so . . . I love him so . . ." All this happened in an instant. And the following minutes brought this: the young girl spoke more and more quietly, like someone who is falling further and further back; the words that just now had been streaming so colorful and proud from her lips crept naked and aimless into the darkness, they felt shame, while her eyes fixed emptily on something down below and gradually went out. There was a stirring. The gazes of the listeners followed hers, and for a second the great, rigid eye of Bohush held all of them trapped. Only for a second — then horror came over them, they rose up like rebellious slaves, the crowd fled with agitated whispers and wild curses into the depths of the passageway, and the light leapt at Bohush's face like a yellow cat. He awoke and quivered. "Rezek!" he cried.

The other leaned over him.

"Bohush, you dog! Are you spying?" he screeched.

Bohush rolled his eyes. He was afraid of the student.

"Are you spying?" he roared.

"Rezek!" roared the cripple even more loudly out of the depths of his fear. Nothing else occurred to him than this name. At the same time his position in the tight hole grew painful, and he felt tears of despair coming on. Then the student helped him up, and immediately he regretted his faintheartedness, remembered his plans, and said with grossly miscarried consideration, "I know everything." (He meant by this the two angry hands of the girl.) "So you were eavesdropping?" the student threatened anew. Bohush dared, not without anxiety, "Rezek, now, Rezek — don't be like this — please, don't be like this. Don't I count too, don't I? I do understand this, don't I? After all I'm with you too — with all my heart." The student regarded him with relentless pressure, and the hunchback became completely helpless under this penetrating, divining stare. He said the same thing a few times more before the means of escape occurred to him: "Without me you wouldn't have found this at all." He meant the cellar. "I knew you could make use of it — and for what," he stressed with feigned craftiness. And the student let himself be deceived. He said with curt decisiveness, "Your hand!" and "Keep quiet." With a certain self-assurance the hunchback laid his stubby fingers in the fanatic's hand; his handshake was without agreement, without emphasis. He knew himself the victor and got ready to set conditions. Expansively he began: he too would speak down here, among them, for the nation and for freedom. Oh, he had really significant plans. Only Rezek must assure him that he might speak here. "Yes," said the student and stressed once more, "Keep quiet!" Bohush nodded past this indifferently and demanded, "So, it's certain — I will speak here?" The other put him off with promises and pushed him toward the door. He evidently didn't fear this cripple much, much less hope for anything from him; he was simply a nuisance. From the stairs he called him back once more. He said for the third time, "Keep quiet," and proffered the grinning fellow something. At first Bohush wanted to reach for it — then he recognized the hard, cruel hand of the student and, projecting out of the threatening fist, a thin, long, sharp knife, along the blade of which the light of the lantern flowed like flaccid blood. And as hard as Bohush tried, he could no longer find his smile. He forced a despairing grimace and, shivering, ascended the steps to his flat. It was near morning.

Since then Bohush couldn't get a night's sleep. He waited day and night for Rezek to call him, and brooded over all that he would have to say then. So many, many things! The most refined things mingled in his fantasies with the crudest ones, and if it seemed to him *now* that he must speak about how one might help poor orphans get a start in life, in the next second he was convinced that he would counsel those down there, that he would command them, to storm churches and palaces. Yes, above all the churches! But always, whatever his speech was about, he saw himself as the midpoint of this group, as the master whom the lovely Carla and many strong young men obeyed respectfully and blindly. He felt like one who had been misjudged for a long time, who was finally claiming his honor and his right to speak, and he passed through the shorelessness of his time, in which night and day had melted together into a uniform gray dusk, filled with the desire to steer them all to this contemplation of his personality. His faithless saint had, like a coward, protected herself from his love behind eternal walls, and from his revenge; but to Frantishka, who would surely also hear his praises soon from Carla's mouth, he would grant the opportunity of attaining his forgiveness. He considered whether he should look her up, and finally wrote a letter piece by piece, over the course of two nights and three days, to his unworthy beloved. His wheedling and immaculate clerk's handwriting virtually ran wild in these pages. Most of the letters looked like boisterous caricatures of the writer, even attesting superfluously to their madness with clothes and caps of a strange sort, and, each behind the back of the next, mocking and deriding one another. In the first section of this expansive epistle he assured her, quite in the manner of medieval sovereigns, of his good and be- nevolent disposition; in the second he told her in strange, endless, and extremely convoluted images of the significance of his secret mission; and in the third he promised: "Since, however, the great secrecy and the indescribable importance of my duties render it, to my deepest regret, completely impossible and impracticable for me to allow you to par- ticipate in the assembly which is to help establish the freedom of my nation and my own renown, I invite you, on the———(here an early date was specified) to visit me at six or seven o'clock in the evening. Before you and my mother I will then speak, as much as I may speak without being a traitor, not to individuals, because I do not fear them, but to the glorious, exalted and just cause . . ." — and this tedious invitation was signed — this flowed more or less of itself from the overexerted pen — "King Bohush. Delivered in Prague."

As the hunchback read this through once more, he had to smile, and he was on the point of destroying the page. Then he thought: no, it's at least a good joke, it certainly is that, sealed the epistle and carried it to the post himself. When he heard it fall in the box, he breathed a deep sigh of relief.

Frantishka hadn't given any answer; but actually Bohush hadn't even expected that. He was convinced that she would come and that, almost humbled, she would find the new Bohush, whose friendship no doubt seemed to her now a great and undeserved gift. Slowly and hesitatingly he would forgive her, and then they would surely not go to the Malvazinka anymore on Sundays, but somewhere they could let themselves be seen, among crowds of people in the Royal Garden, or into the Star.[33]

All of this Bohush thought about only very fleetingly in the few pauses in which the great matter did not occupy him, which by this time had come to be his duty, his life. It was an exhausting duty to think all at once these many important things that he had thought little by little during the lean years, to survey all of them at once and then to pronounce them in order. There was such a throng of opinions, memories, and plans in him that a whole swarm always wanted to get by his lips, wild and reckless like people fleeing a burning theater. Then Bohush put on a stern expression

---

33. Two famous public parks. The Royal Garden, north of the castle, was laid out for Ferdinand I beginning in 1634. The "Star" is the park containing the Star Summer Palace, built for Ferdinand of Tyrol in 1555 and 1556 in the western part of the city near White Mountain. Its floorplan is based on a six-pointed star.

and commanded haughtily, "Quiet — one after the other. Everyone will have a turn." And on just these occasions it happened that the whole crowd suddenly vanished, simply melted away, and Bohush was completely void in his head and in no condition to think, let alone say, anything. Only when he had drunk a few glasses of hot *czay* did the colorful rabble reappear, and the hunchback rejoiced and laughed until his eyes were full of tears. The restlessness of his character had meanwhile grown steadily greater. He read a lot in newspapers and old books, scribbled whole notebooks full of his ludicrous letters, and, right in the middle of these occupations, no matter if day or night, in a café or in a church, rarely at home, he slept a few moments of fleeting sleep, out of which he soon sprang up as if alarmed.

So the morning of the day neared on which Bohush had promised the evening address before his mother and Frantishka, neither of whom was allowed to take part in his actual triumph. His night had been passed in various restaurants and taverns, and now he crept along beside the houses, exhausted and bleary-eyed, staring stupidly and apathetically into the dense, rosy morning mist of the spring day. Few people passed him. At the Powder Tower[34] two servant girls came toward him with large shopping baskets, laughing and chattering, their eyes so fresh and awake, their dresses and aprons still stiff from pure newness. A bit further on two infantry soldiers overtook him. They strode smartly; their gait beat out a joyous rhythm on the pavement, and the buttons on their uniforms stole the sun's early rays and cast them boldly into the sleepy eyes of Bohush. Then some mischievous baker's boy whistled into the hunchback's face

---

34. The Powder Tower is a Gothic arch at the intersection of Na příkopě ("am Graben"), Hybernská (Hybernergasse), and Celetná (Zeltnergasse). It was begun in 1475 in honour of King Vladislav Jagellon as one of the gates in the fortifications of the Old Town, and gained its name when it was used as a storehouse for gunpowder in the late seventeenth century. Between 1875 and 1886 it was reconstructed in neo-Gothic style.

and laughed loudly after him, and a policeman sang something or other to himself, while the plumes on his hat waved a little. The metal cages of shops clattered open, and the reflecting panes gave themselves wholly to the sun and blazed with white flames. Through this fresh, joyous revival the hunchback crept, pale, ruined, with a badly wrinkled shirt and dirty clothes; he was like a poisonous, hideous toad that one discovers in the middle of sweet-smelling flower beds. He was entirely oblivious of all the brightness, too, except that it bothered him; perhaps he hardly knew that it was springtime and morning. Meanwhile, the more this morning matured, the more it became apparent that everyone was displaying a certain uneasiness. People who used to exchange greetings daily at this hour, without speaking with one another, halted, put on worried or astonished expressions, shrugged their shoulders, and finally shook hands with a certain conventional appreciation, only to be stopped again ten paces further on. Evidently one felt the need to inform others of something that concerned and interested them all. At the corner of Ferdinand Street a porter was reading out a section of the *Czesky Curir*[35] to a circle of men and servant girls, and a bit further on an elderly gentleman stepped out of a coffeehouse and said to his companion in German, "Those are extremely dangerous people. One should . . ." What one should do could no longer be made out. The gentleman went on quite self-confidently on very shiny shoes, and the young one beside him nodded at every word, confirming it loyally; he seemed to be entirely of the same opinion. When Bohush came into the vicinity of the National, he recognized Norinski through a window; he seemed to be explaining something in his heroic manner to the others, who could not be seen. The hunchback hesitated for a while. Then, instead of entering, he went down along the quay toward his flat. He was tired.

35. Rilke's name for the illustrated journal *Pražský kurýr*, or *Prague Courier*.

Meanwhile Norinski had come to an end. He emptied his coffee with an extravagant gesture — it might have been a cup of hemlock — and said grandly, "None of you will say that I am not a good Czech. And I will lose no opportunity to convince the wretched Germans of the contrary as well. Just let one of them come to me. I'll show the gentleman what's what. But you mustn't make so much of these stories. That's nothing. Those are childish pranks, you can take my word for it." With this he got up without paying for his breakfast, made presents of the magnanimous three-act handshakes and, holding his head high, betook himself to his dressing room. Those who were left shifted together intimately, and Karás began to read out the various very brief newspaper articles that related to the incident. All said approximately the same thing: the police, acting on the advice of a woman, had been put on the track of a band of young people, students and apprentices, who were holding secret meetings in the cellar areas of a house in Hieronymus Street, at which the order of business was highly treasonable speeches. It was interesting to emphasize that girls too were said to have taken part in these meetings. And German papers rejoiced, moreover, about the destruction of this infamous nest of criminals, and regretted only that, through the sullen silence of those comrades taken into custody, the spiritual head of this conspiracy was not yet in the hands of the public security forces, which event, however, thanks to the excellent experience and keen-sightedness of the police force, was surely not far off. And, the most German of the newspapers added further, they hoped that one would finally set a long-awaited example by these young criminals and archtraitors and proceed with ruthless severity. All of this was read out in the National. Schileder was honestly indignant; he said something about the courage of the young people and about the fact that they did not just produce words, fine words, but also intended to act. He couldn't express it very well and fell silent, intimidated, when he found no overly animated assent. All of them did nod for a moment, his friends, and lay some little word, like an embarrassed alms, in the hand of justice. But, after all — they all looked around — they were so temptingly alone that one *could* make a few confessions. Pátek condemned in short order this cavern romanticism, which after all wasn't even justified in novels anymore, and the lyric poet Machal, who only had a very uncertain idea of what had taken place, yawned and threw in, between two attempts at yawns, that the whole thing seemed to him brutal, terribly brutal. Karás, who felt more cosmopolitan every day, gave a longer speech, during which his Adam's apple climbed up and down like a tree frog racked by indecision. His conclusion was that, for external purposes, because of the circumstances, one must with all one's resources uphold the view that these young people were not only martyrs to their cause, but also the fallen heroes of a national affair, yet that he himself — here — had no choice but to condemn these immaturities — yes, immaturities! — of half-grown youths. After all, they were too well-educated for that; they knew, of course, that one could sooner protect one's rights through major nationalistic activities in life and in the political arena (an expression that Karás also employed consistently in his feuilletons) than through such improprieties. He must have had a few more fluent sentences in reserve, but he suddenly stopped. He himself didn't know why. The others looked up, and there stood Rezek in front of them. The student, his dark eyes burning in his wan face, ignored the hands that they stretched toward him. Perhaps he had heard the critic's last words, but he did not reply; instead, he sat down quietly in his usual place and drank his *czay*. His hard hands trembled a bit. No one dared speak. At last Pátek began to talk about a new book, and the artists lost themselves completely in this discussion. It had to do with some novellas in the style of Maupassant that a young colleague wished to publish. There were still a few difficulties with the question of money and in other matters of publication, and they were discussing whether they should come to the author's aid. The powerful Karás was not very inclined to. Pátek shouted indignantly: "But, listen, this is a national affair!"

Rezek stood up with an icy smile. "Are you Czechs?" he asked.[36]

Without speaking, they all looked disconcertedly at one another. Schileder had stood up.

"Are you Czechs?" repeated the student.

Karás calmed him: "What's got into you, Rezek? Don't provoke us."

"But you are mature? Are you not?" he continued. "Mature and finished."

"He's drunk," Machal whispered contemptuously.

Rezek clenched his fists. But he restrained himself. "I know you are in the habit of conceiving righteous indignation for common drunkenness. I know. But I just want to tell you, the nation is *not* mature, and if you feel so finished, then you are its enemies, you are traitors."

"I am an officer," Pátek said in an anxious voice as he stepped forward.

Rezek held his fist in front of his face and, without a word, walked past him out of the room.

Bohush couldn't expect Frantishka before six or seven o'clock, as he had appointed in his letter. All the same, he wondered from three o'clock on why his beloved still didn't come; toward four he was on the point of going to fetch her, and he gave up the idea unwillingly and hesitatingly out of pride or for some other reason. He ran about restlessly, hands behind his back, in the small rooms, the closely packed heirlooms that they'd taken along in excessive measure out of the porter's lodge making this to and fro sub-

36. The provocative nature of Rezek's question lies partly in the fact that he suddenly uses the familiar form of address (*ihr*), whereas the artists normally address each other with the formal pronoun *Sie*.

stantially more difficult. Only from time to time did he stop by the window, at which a little old woman sat sewing.

"Mother," he finally uttered in agony, "you must go and get her!"

The old woman nodded, lifted the large round glasses from her eyes and nodded. She didn't hesitate for a moment: naturally, she must go and get Frantishka. And she exchanged the bonnet for a hat and drew a good yellow shawl about her crooked shoulders. "You can say you were just passing by, you . . . Oh God — well, you just happened to be passing by. Couldn't you? Why couldn't you just accidentally pass by there? Surely lots of people pass by there." Bohush laughed abortively. "Well, come on," he started up in impatient fury, "can you do that?" Mrs. Bohush nodded, completely intimidated. "You know, I'll go to the church first, next door. Then I can say I've been in the church . . ." Still she hesitated. Bohush had long since begun to think about other things. He hardly saw the old woman any more and was almost astonished when, in the course of his rambling back and forth, he found himself standing in front of her. The yellow cloth was unbearably harsh in the afternoon sun. They gazed at each other for a while in silence, these two small, stunted individuals. Then the old woman pattered to the door, nodding and nodding. Suddenly Bohush was beside her. "*Maminko,*"[37] he said, and his voice was like that of a sick child. And the old, cowed woman understood. She grew, she became rich, she became a mother. It was this one quiet word that made her so. All the anxiety in her was at once kindness, and she who had just now looked so unprotected and helpless was mighty as she gently spread her arms, and for Bohush it was like coming home. He nestled his great, heavy, ringing head against her breast, he closed his burning eyes, he sank into this endless, deep love. He was silent. And then something inside him began to cry. He

37. "Mother dear."

heard precisely how it started up. It must be very deep inside him, it was so quiet. It didn't hurt, either. And then he opened his eyes in curiosity; he had to see where the crying was. And look: it wasn't even crying inside him; it was his mother. Then Bohush couldn't close his eyelids any more: tears lurked behind them, many tears.

All at once it was so solemn in the room. The objects around the two wretched people took on a gleam that they had never possessed, not even in their ducal days. Each little pitcher, each little glass in the stiff sideboard all at once had its own light and paraded with it and wanted to play at being a star. One can imagine that it became very bright in the room.

Then the clock struck, cautiously, as if it regretted having to do so. But it did strike, five times, and the mother left.

"Where to?" the hunchback asked anxiously.

"I must get Frantishka." Then Bohush remembered everything. He hesitated and then said almost sadly, "Oh, yes, you must get Frantishka."

That was the farewell.

When Bohush was alone, he began again his nervous and perplexed pacing. Here and there, as if in passing, he righted something, swept the dust from the tabletop and lost himself unintentionally in the ordering of his writings and books. In doing so he became quite warm. And when he caught sight of his burning face somewhere in a mirror, he was astonished. He was wearing, nestled around his shoulders, his mother's harsh yellow silk shawl. That was comical. He wanted to laugh, but forgot to, and with involuntary motions of contentment he buried his back even further in the soft folds. He felt tired; in the sitting room he let himself fall, heavy and broad, onto the flowered cushions of the stiff settee, which, together with the oval table, just filled the middle of the room. He thought and thought.

The poor, solemn settee complained under him. He sprang up, smoothed the crocheted dust covers with a certain tenderness, and settled in one of the chairs that stood off to the side. His face, which could sometimes be boyish, now aged from minute to minute under the influence of his strained meditation; it was virtually eaten away by the wrinkles that crawled over it and bored their way in like caterpillars into a diseased fruit. Was he really sure of everything he was going to say? A vague anxiety hung over him. He felt so abandoned, dizzy, like one who has been forgotten up on a high tower. He felt around for something to hold on to. And in the next while he fancied that he was even disturbing the order, the solemn order of the room, by waiting in *this* spot. He was shocked at his audacity. He crept further and further back and huddled finally on a high-legged stool in the corner of the room, close to the door. Then stillness came over him. He thought: So, now it's over; I've already said it all, and yet he knew that he had only wept, and that is something different from a speech, weeping like that. Nevertheless, he persisted stubbornly: I've said it all, my mother knows all — "and you too" he finished aloud, seeking the eyes of the yellow cat that was coming slowly and slyly toward him out of the opposite corner. No claw grated on the gleaming brown floorboards. Soundlessly the animal came closer, it grew large, it grew larger, and when it was so large that Bohush could no longer see past it into the still, solemn room, then he slept. And he must have dreamed. For he said in a voice that sounded a long way off, "That is it, Rezek, if you please — that is the secret. The painter must paint the nation and say to it: you are beautiful." Then his head fell forward, and he forced it up again only with difficulty. "The poet must compose the nation and say to it: you are beautiful." He sighed in his dream. "To be beautiful, that's it." Then a smile began at the corners of his mouth, a good, pious smile, which spread over the face of the sleeper and made it young again. He still breathed: "I will never betray it," and then his dream became so deep that no word of it rose to his lips any longer.

The door opened. The hunchback, however, opened his eyes only when Rezek gripped him roughly at the throat and screeched close by: "Did you keep quiet?" Bohush felt the words very hot on his cheek. His hands fended off convulsively, but there was still no understanding in his eyes. They still smiled. They smiled at the dreadful avenger until they died. And then the yellow cloth slid over the wretched body and covered up Bohush and his secret.

The Siblings

At NOON THE NEW TENANTS had moved into the old house across from the Maltese church,[1] three flights up, and until evening all that was known was that they had brought with them unusually large pieces of furniture, which had nearly got stuck in the tight turns of the winding staircase. And the old, bleary-eyed peddler-woman who sat nearby under the dark stone arcades could hardly get over the thought of the huge oaken wardrobes, and she besought the neighbors to take her word for it that they had been "real upperclass" wardrobes. This assurance brought about an unusual restlessness that kept the many small factions in that particular house in suspense. Every other minute an untidy woman would emerge from one or another of the white enameled doors, on each of which a few grimy visiting cards crowded around a name plate of tin or glass; she would listen at the stairs and draw back in embarrassment when she came upon other listeners already there, who likewise started to pull back in alarm, until the like-minded souls recognized one another and only whetted their starving curiosity even more with dark speculations.

But suddenly the female occupants were drawn out of the narrow stairwell, which rose up like a spinal column through the masonry, toward the courtyard windows. Deep down in the tubular courtyard, as at the bottom of a well, a barrel organ gaspingly took up the tune from the *Student Prince*,[2] and at the same time — though no one knew where they came from — there were already a few children there performing a wild and curious dance around the old tippler. But after some tortured groaning the notes emerged out of the dry throats of the organ like belches; they seemed to

1. The Maltese church of Our Lady-below-the-Chain was founded in 1160 as part of the monastery of the Knights of Malta and was remodeled in the fourteenth century. Its Gothic facade is solid and rather bleak. The "old house" on the opposite side of the street is the former Palais Doudlebský-Sterneck on Lázeňská (Badgasse).
2. *Der Bettelstudent,* an 1882 operetta by Karl Millöcker.

rush upward and tug like invisible lassos at the various necks
that grew to quite incredible lengths out of every opening
and kitchen window and broke up the bareness of the walls
like some bizarre architectural ornamentation. The women
who greeted each other from all sides looked alike enough
in the dusk to be mistaken for one another; as if in cautious
camouflage, their faces all seemed to have taken on the indescribable off-color of the masonry, and gesture and voice
too manifested such a surprising uniformity that they might
have been taken for component organs of this house rather
than free-moving individuals. One could easily believe that
the attentiveness of the many heads was directed to the pitiful
barrel organ, for some were even nodding along with the
rhythm; but in reality all the eyes gravitated very gently
toward the third-floor kitchen window, and several credulous ears thought to hear its latch click. But it was only the
barrel organ, which had exhausted itself with a galop, to
which a small black pinscher had howled an accompaniment;
the minstrel roared his thanks and shuffled off with pon-
derous steps. The bright swarm of children followed along
behind him like a chain, and all at once everyone sensed the
stillness and dark of the musty courtyard. But just at this
extraordinarily attentive moment the longed-for window
opened almost inaudibly, and the old servant Rosalka[3]
leaned a long way out. Almost all the heads dove down;
only one pert, impatient voice cried out, "So, have you finished moving in by now?" The maid Rosalka only nodded,
and just as the barrel organ quietly took up some very plain-
tive tune at one of the next houses, the old woman sat down
like a large, mournful bird in the black window and let piece
after piece of the life history of her employers drop carelessly
down, as if they were potato peelings, into the hearkening
courtyard. And even though there was no one to be seen at

---

3. Rosalka may be Rilke's Slavic version of the name Rosalie, though it is
also reminiscent of the Czech name Rusalka, meaning (ironically) water nymph.

the windows now, still none of her long-drawn phrases was lost to the walls, from which an encouraging question now and again ascended. An hour later, when they tolled the Ave at the Maltese church, even the old peddler-woman under the arcades knew the entire fate of the forester's widow Josephine Wanka and her two children, and she bestowed it on the last of her daily customers, the court-of-chancery clerk Jerabek and the lackey Dvorak, together with the "real upperclass" wardrobes.

But perhaps the old woman's general confession would not even have been necessary to satisfy the women's thirst. For the three individuals who had moved from tiny Krumlov[4] to the capital wore their memories and experiences on their sleeves, as it were, so that one needed only to brush against them to carry a piece away. In part this must have lain in the custom of the small town, in which everyone bedecks himself with his joy and carries his sorrow with him too, as visibly as possible; anyone who is so unwise as not to follow suit has both of them hauled out of his secret hiding place by the merciless hands of his neighbors, and he may see if he recognizes his quiet joy or his still sorrow again in the rumor that hate and mockery have disfigured. In the case of the Wanka family, however, this candor might have its basis first of all in the fact that the most recent and most consequential event of its life still overshadowed it, even though a year had passed since that time. In the females especially one still noticed the traces left by fate, one seemed to see the marks of its brutal clutches in their faces, and one heard the fear that was always somewhere in the background of their voices, waiting to spread, suddenly and for no reason, over every word. Only the twenty-year-old son, Zdenko, had something serious and reserved in his

4. Krumlov (Krummau in German) is an old town on the Vltava River in southern Bohemia. In 1899 it had a population of 8,331, most of whom were German.

austere visage that quickly robbed him of all sympathy; only
the fact that (as was already heard in the course of these first
days) he was a student of medicine caused him to be granted,
in place of sympathy, a certain grudging respect, which he
nevertheless seemed not to notice or else to reject. But even
if the women continually betrayed themselves in their behavior, they retained, all the same, a coolness toward their
obliging housemates, and since that first day, weeks had
passed without one of the neighbor women having entered
the rooms of the forester's widow. Thanks to the difficulty
of achieving this, it had gradually become a goal that they
all vied to attain; they spared no strategem, and well into
the late evening hours they came to borrow from the Wankas
a sugar mortar or a corkscrew, which they misplaced remarkably often, or ultimately the key to the attic, things that
they generally carried off along with the vexation of not
having seen past the threshold of the living room.

This hopeless obstinacy bore no relation to the original
confessions of the old servant, and it was understandable
that they had the highest hopes of her cooperation; yet even
she seemed to become more reticent and mistrustful. When
urged, she would always begin to retell the one story that
everyone long since knew, about the March morning on
which the woodsmen had brought the gamekeeper Joachim
Wanka home out of the forest, shot dead by poachers. And
that his face was filled with rigid fury and dark as it lay
there, as if completely shaded by the bushy brows, and how
his fists would not unclench, not even in the flood of tears,
so that the forester would surely have a hard time of it —
eventually — on Judgment Day, to act as if he had lain there
the whole time with piously folded hands. Then the old
woman crossed herself with a habitual, chance motion and
assured them excessively that she had known of the whole
calamity long before through dreams and signs and also
from the fact that Sir Julius Caesar had walked about again

in Krumlov Castle,[5] and that the castellan had had the Emperor Rudolph[6] sit across from him in an armchair, head in his hands, gazing across the nighttime Vltava valley into the stars.

Anyone who was unwilling to believe in such things was dismissed by old Rosalka without further ado, for she held this to be a lack of education and experience and one of the many detrimental consequences of that culture that was making ever more powerful inroads "in the big city." Also, in the evenings, when Mrs. Wanka seemed to be carrying on really serious and considered conversations with her son, she could not help beckoning the daughter, Luisa, who sat by so very superfluously with great, lost eyes, secretly into the kitchen and warning her about the sinful mouths of the heretics who had no respect for anything anymore — not for a graveyard and not for midnight, no, not even for both together. And in a very short time that atmosphere was conjured up in which the old woman felt at home: the surrounding objects, from the stiff kitchen cabinet to the plump washtub, which just now had stood there so soberly, all at once began to listen in, and it was as if they edged closer and closer to the two women so as not to lose a word of Rosalka's. Sounds as of footsteps awoke, and without any reason one of the old tin pans giggled: "plink!" Then the maid stopped short, and with pounding hearts both of them followed the silvery sound: it was as if an invisible clock had struck some significant hour. Some-

---

5. Krumlov Castle, located on a steep cliff overlooking the Vltava River, is the second-largest castle in Bohemia, next to Prague Castle. According to legend, a young woman who was being chased by Sir Julius Caesar, the mad son of Emperor Rudolph II, threw herself out of the window of the castle's tower room.

6. Rudolph II, who reigned as both King of Bohemia and Holy Roman Emperor from 1566 to 1611, resided in Prague from the year 1583. He made the city into a center of art, culture, science, and trade; during this era it became known as "Golden Prague."

times the old kitchen lamp, as if in complicity with Rosalka, went out just as they were listening so attentively, and the sated dusk grew heavy and close with a thousand reeling possibilities. Luisa, who always sat utterly mute in a corner, became smaller and smaller in relation to these powers; she seemed to dissolve and leave nothing behind except two great fearful eyes, which followed the ghostly figures with a sort of credulous trust. Then it was as if she were in the great ballroom of Krumlov Castle, the walls of which are painted right up to the arched, echoing ceiling with life-size figures.[7] A French painter is said to have composed these carnival groups many hundreds of years ago so skillfully, in such rich and surprising variety that — even in the light of day — more and more new, fantastically costumed guests appear to surface behind each of the figures. Only in Krumlov do they know for certain that this lies not in the merit of the painter, but in the strange fact that at a certain hour the knights and ladies begin to awaken, to repeat the drama of that one distant night. Stepping out of the walls, they fill the room with their shimmering billows. Until the huge grenadiers at the ballroom doors ram their halberds hard on the ground: then the rows come to order. A sound of

7. The most famous attraction of Krumlov Castle is the ballroom, decorated by the Swabian-born artist Joseph Lederer in 1748 with elaborate frescoes inspired by figures from the masquerade and the *commedia dell'arte*. Rilke's visit to the castle became a recurring motif in his early work. In the 1895 story "Böhmische Schlendertage" ("Bohemian Rambles"), he describes the impression made by the ballroom: "It is one of a kind. The entire walls are covered with larger-than-life figures, painted with spirited irony. There one sees knights and lords, noble ladies and dignified matrons, dwarves and giants, harlequins and magicians in a colorful, teeming throng. Musicians play in the galleries, ladies look on from their boxes, and at the door two huge, smart grenadiers keep a stern watch. The wealth of figures and their wonderful, simple plasticity make a downright stunning impression" (*Sämtliche Werke*, vol. 6, 290). The story of the girl who throws herself from the tower room of Krumlov Castle was the subject of an unpublished one-act play entitled *Das Thurmzimmer* (*The Tower Room*), which Rilke wrote in 1895. In 1898 he published another prose sketch entitled "Masken" ("Masks") in the journal *Ver Sacrum*, which is incorporated almost verbatim into "The Siblings" at this point.

thunder rolls over them. With his wild black team of six, Prince Julius Caesar, natural son of Rudolph II, has ridden up the projecting ramp, and barely a heartbeat later he stands, black and slim, in the midst of the guests who make deep, deep bows — like a cypress in a waving wheat field. Then the music mingles the multitude, a foreign music that seems to arise with the rustling of the costly gowns and, growing, rises broad and roaring out of the masses, like the melody of an ocean. Here and there the prince parts with a nod the shining waves, disappears between them, steps proudly out of them in the far corner, lets his shining smile glide over them like a sudden ray of sunlight and hurls a bright high-spirited phrase, like an exquisite ring that they all chase after, into the middle of the billows. And amid the wilder, wallowing to and fro grows the secret lust. At the side of a silver knight the prince recognizes a pale young lady in blue, and at once feels love for her, hate for her escort. Both are red and rash within him. And he must have made the silver knight a king, for crimson flows down over the shiny armor, ever broader and bloodier, until he breaks down wordlessly under the burden of the princely robe: "It happens to many a king," the prince laughs into his dying eyes. Then the festive figures grow rigid with horror and pale slowly and anxiously back into the extinguishing walls, and like a sallow, rocky shore the abandoned room rises out of the last lustrous waves. Only Julius Caesar stays behind, and the greedy glow of his ardent eyes singes the pale young lady's senses. But as he tries to grasp her, she tears herself away from his mastering gaze and flees into the black, echoing room; her light gown of blue silk remains, tattered, like a fragment of moonlight in the prince's wild fingers, and he winds it around his neck and chokes himself with it. Then he feels his way after her into the night and suddenly gives a shout of joy. He hears that she has discovered the little concealed door and he knows that now she is his, because from there only a single path exists, the narrow tower stairs that open into the small, fragrant, round chamber, high in the Vltava tower. With wanton haste he is after her, always after her; he cannot hear her driven step, yet he sees her like a gleam before him at each turn of the stair. He lays hold of her again, and now he holds the delicate, fear-warmed slip in his hand, only the slip; it is cool on his lips and cheeks. He swoons, and as he kisses his prize he leans hesitatingly against the wall. Then with three, four tigerlike leaps he appears at the door of the tower room — and freezes: high in the night the pure white body, naked, rises up, as if it had blossomed from the window ledge. Both are motionless. But then, before he can think, two bright, childishly delicate arms rise into the stars as if to become wings, something goes out in front of him, and before the high arch of the window there is nothing except hollow, howling night and a cry . . .

— — — — — — — — — — — — — — — — — — — —

"And you're really eighteen?" said Zdenko as he bent over his frightened, weeping little sister, who, very small and timid, was all but lost in the corner of the kitchen. "So your old ghosts follow you even here, to Prague? Or has Rosalka brought them along in her pots and pans?" The old servant turned away sulking. "Yes," Luisa hesitated, "yes," and she drew a halting breath, "at first, when we came here, I thought I was rid of them. When I saw the bright houses and the broad streets, I felt very free and happy; but here in the Lesser Town it's almost worse than back home. Isn't it?" The girl looked around slowly. But Zdenko pulled her after him into the bright living room. "It's just as I said," he called to his mother, "while we sit here talking, she's already back out there with the old witch and all upset by the same old nonsense." Mrs. Josephine quietly shook her head with its broad, gray temples and said, "When will you ever learn some sense, child?" She sewed silently on at pieces of white linen, and much more work lay waiting in the basket beside her. Yet after a while the widow laid her bepricked fingers in her lap and gazed into her daughter's face. Blinded by the bright lamp, Luisa had closed her eyes, and there were still such distinct traces of fear in her delicate, pale little face that the mother was shocked. All at once it struck her how weak and willowy the girl was, and whether she would ever have enough strength one day to stand and face life without any succor and support. The benevolent, pale blue eyes of the mother clouded with tears — but that might also be caused by exertion, for plain sewing is a tedious occupation, and Mrs. Wanka's eyelids were always slightly reddened by it. Luisa, who must have felt the gaze, set about after a while to help her mother. So both women were bent over the linen, and the hanging lamp lit up harshly the gray and blonde heads. Now Zdenko said: "I don't know, I always fancy that Luisa stayed so small just out of awe. Really. That's possible. If a person always, from a very young age, sees only such large things as she has — just think of the castle on the steep cliff, those high courtyards, the great cannons on the entrenchments, and finally in the rooms — chairs and pictures and vases — everything made as if for giants — then he either grows after these objects . . ." (Mrs. Wanka looked into her son's face with a smile and then sewed eagerly on) "or he completely loses all courage to grow after them. For he must think to himself: I'll never get that big. And with all this gazing and wondering the days pass by, and one forgets about oneself and forgets that these objects really only set an example, after all. Don't you think so, Luisa?"

"Maybe," his sister nodded, without interrupting her work.

"I once felt it too, you know, that that can oppress one — as a boy." Zdenko stared beyond the women blankly. "But then at some point the jolt comes, when one stands on one's toes in front of all that, instead of kneeling down before it, and when one has come that far, it's not very long until one can look beyond it. And believe me, that makes all the difference. Just always looking at things from above.

Whoever stands at the highest point is always master. I've always had a very clear idea of what it is that makes our time so confused and so insecure, but now that I'm here in the city and see lots of people, I know it: it's that no one stands over them. You tell me that's wrong: over the city is the mayor and over him the governor, and he has to look up a good bit again to the king and the king to the emperor and he to the pope. But the pope, despite his triply tall crown, still doesn't reach up as far as the Good Lord, you say. I think that comes because people usually look at the thing from the wrong end. It seems to me that very deep down is the Good Lord and a little over him the pope and so forth. But at the top are the people. Only the people are not one, they are many; they push and shove one another, and one of them eclipses the sun for someone else. So I always think they should lift someone or other up to a height from time to time, not too high (he could easily fall down to where the king is, or the emperor) but still so that he feels their strong and loyal shoulders under him and can look out over their heads for a while in quiet reflection. Then when he is standing among them again it will be as if he'd returned from his homeland, and he'll be able to tell his brothers where the sun rises and how long it might take to get there — and more things of that sort. But this way . . ." Zdenko covered his eyes with his hand. Then he stood up suddenly. "Well, leave that drudgery alone now and go to bed; it's late. The lamp is about to go out too." His voice was rough. He noticed only now that Luisa was no longer sitting there bent over the white stuff; her eyes burned toward him, great and shining as never before. And, strange to say, he saw himself in those eyes and straightened up proud and strong as before a mirror.

His mother, though, sewed uninterruptedly with brisk, tireless toil, and Zdenko quite suddenly felt the need to go to her and kiss her hands.

*   *   *

It wasn't mistrust that had rendered the maid Rosalka still and reticent toward her housemates. That often happens to elderly people when, driven out of the familiar domesticity of their provincial town, they must make their way in a new place; they can't adapt themselves to the larger scale and are as if displaced from a close chamber into an echoing hall, in which their most private utterances are repeated aloud as if by invisible choirs, while their many vehement gestures seem to lose themselves in the latitudes of this apathetic space. At first they enjoy the novelty of this, but soon they perceive it as an exertion, which, without sufficient reward, has a discouraging effect, and one morning they begin to let their hands lie in their laps and their words on their tongues. For it must be added that people in the country are a good deal more modest. There it is enough to have had one really substantial misfortune in order to draw on the respectful sympathy of acquaintances like a lifelong pension for all time, up to the last blessed day. But "in the big city" (sulked the old woman) to stay halfway on top, one is supposed to lose a father at least once a week and to fall down the stairs or out of the window every three weeks. With sorrowful eyes she thought back on her "status" in Krumlov and couldn't forgive her employers for having moved to Prague to allow Zdenko to attend the university. She granted that the forester's widow now had to go "into service" herself a few times a week to supplement her small pension and the royal allowance of the Schwarzenbergs through plain sewing, by that amount which the new household and the education of her son required. She knew, too, that Mrs. Wanka would sacrifice everything for her son and that she had the secret wish of seeing him a "learned doctor," which seemed to Rosalka like the improper ambition of an unbridled arrogance, because of which it was advisable to cross oneself three times.

This effort of the widow's was perceived differently in the house of Mrs. Retired Colonel Meering von Meerhelm, where the forester's widow mended the fine linen once each week, namely on Monday, which was wash day. For Mrs. Charlotte Meering praised the mother's eagerness and criticized only the fact that Zdenko Wanka had entered the Bohemian rather than the German university.[8] This glaring mistake was the reason that one could never invite him into the house. In vain the widow assured her that it had been done entirely in the spirit of her poor late husband, who had been a good Czech; the colonel's wife only smiled politely, "not being able," as she expressed herself to her husband, "to understand the limited outlook of these people." Luisa, on the other hand, was sometimes allowed to come to pick up her mother, and, if she promised to speak only German, to "play" for ten minutes with the Meering children, fifteen-year-old Rangen and Lizzie, who was about three years younger. The result was of course always the opposite; that is, the two siblings hurled themselves on the shy and timid girl and began to push and shove her like some inanimate object, until Mrs. von Meering usually entered the door of the nursery just at the moment when Luisa, bound to a wardrobe, represented a white sacrifice, while her offspring leapt around her with wild howls of victory, Indian style. So it was not surprising that Luisa in no way looked forward to these visits and was grateful when her mother permitted her to wait in the entrance hall or in the street. Sometimes the Colonel would happen by her on his way home and, preferring to avoid the horrors of wash day, would pause in front of the girl a moment longer. The small, rather plump man, who wore a great feeling of worth on the inside and a great medal on the outside of his chest,

---

8. Charles-Ferdinand University in Prague was founded in 1348 by Emperor Charles IV and was the first university in central Europe. In 1882 the university began to hold separate German and Czech classes, and by 1891 it was formally divided into a German and a Czech (Bohemian) school.

puffed up his moustache with a certain well-being and always prefaced the short conversation this way:

"Waiting for Mr. Bridegroom, my dear young lady?"

At this Luisa would always turn as red as the poor lighting in the street required. The old gentleman took pleasure in that, and from one time to the next he recognized ever more clearly the pricelessness of his joke, which he liked to repeat to his Lotti over dinner, naturally after the children had gone to bed. Other than this, in any case, he didn't have a lot to say. For there was something dreamy in his character that this example may also illuminate. He considered for more than five years what the nod that he was occasionally given from "upstairs" might mean. He only understood it, of course, much later, when the tireless nodding from higher up had already called forth a kind of storm, which finally blew the Colonel from the dangerous peak of a regimental command gently down into the respectable valley of retirement, in which he now strolled, pondering as before. He was a man who measured the depths of life by the gruesome abysses of old fables and often marveled how high, in spite of all perils, he had climbed on the earthly ladder. But his just disposition didn't impart unreserved recognition to himself alone; he knew how to treat everyone according to his worth and dignity. Since he had learned that the deceased Wanka had been a royal gamekeeper and that Mrs. Josephine, too, had now and then acted as chambermaid in Frauenberg Castle,[9] he liked to see the widow in his house and felt a breath of indirect princely favor exude from this family.

On these Monday evenings, when Mrs. Wanka finally, with tired eyes, passed through the gate of the Meering house, she kissed her daughter, and usually without exchanging a word the two women walked through the lively streets of the New Town toward the stone bridge. Only when they had steered from the noisy Bridge Street into

9. A castle in southern Bohemia that belonged to the Schwarzenberg family.

the narrow, barely lit side alleys did their tongues loosen, and they began to talk quietly and slowly of Zdenko, like two toy clocks dreaming their timorous songs in the middle of the night. Over their conversations lay a loyal, moving tenderness that sounded all the more sincere in that it never descended into the words, but wholly filled the women, beautified their gestures and made their smiles more luminous. Since that evening when Luisa's eyes had so strangely caught fire at her brother's heated words, he had become a different person for her, one who had power; and even if the love that Mrs. Wanka cherished for her son sprang from deeper sources, still mother and daughter understood each other in this quiet and attentive language, and in it, with many words, they said approximately this to one another: he has become a different person.

They were right about that. A joyous excitement had come over the young man. His friendship with the woods and the rustic peace of his paternal home had bestowed gifts on him, again and again, and what was expected from him in return had been so laughably little. When he thought back over the years before his father's death, he was now inclined to believe that he had really known only a single day, which, contented and full, emerged again and again from behind each night, up until the first weighty sorrow — the violent death of his treasured father. Behind that lay something lifeless and empty, that was like stopping to rest, or like forgetting. But right in the middle somewhere — so he perceived it — a door, a gate had then opened, and now they stormed in, nothing but young and colorful days, reaching out their hands to him with impatient pleading. How grateful he was to them for their desire! He stood there like one who has come back home, who hands out gifts on all sides; the things have come from far away, and each recipient knows how to put them to good use. Wanka had the feeling that the whole world was living out of his pocket, and it shouldn't do badly thereby. He could always be found in a

circle of young people to whom he tossed serious and frivolous ideas in colorful disarray, and they all found enough
in them to fill their days and nights. He didn't notice the
aimlessness in these young heads; he himself had no aim,
because he had a thousand of them and thought to grasp
this one today, that one tomorrow. This way of living
brought him into contact with a great number of people,
and he gave himself over to all of them with equal loyalty,
and when he had once again grown thoroughly enthusiastic
over a new thought of his own, then he believed he had to
thank for it these people who stood around him skeptically.
By and by he grew quieter, listened carefully to the objec-
tions as well, and discovered that he was really in no position
to answer them. Gradually he began to realize that all his
enthusiasms were fragments of a great monologue, and this
recognition rendered him much more sober and lonesome.

Now he would sit silently all night long at the table of
regulars in the National Café, which was frequented by men
who were older and more serious than he and whom he
believed to stand at the summit of the race. They were poets
and painters, actors and students. There was something in
the behavior of all of them that had once strongly repelled
him, only he sought to accustom himself to it. After the
theater they found their way together, tired and moody, and
when they exchanged greetings they smiled at one another
sympathetically. Their clothing manifested either a kind of
exaggerated elegance or else a crude neglect, and at first
sight it was difficult to recognize what they had in common.
It took a few glasses of *czay* or Budweiser beer to make it
apparent that the similarity lay in the great pronouncements
that came ever more plentifully and tumultuously from their
lips the later it grew. Nevertheless a distinction was upheld
by the fact that those in modern clothes only laid their words
in front of them on the table, as it were, with the warning
"do not touch," while the others simply tossed them into
the air, let them strike whom they might. Here Wanka heard

the affairs of the "nation" discussed; he learned for the first time about its affliction and need, about its still and inward longing. Shame came over him suddenly as over one who, while laughing, discovers there is a corpse in the house, and he wondered how it could have happened that he hadn't noticed anything at all of this oppression over the many years. He thirsted to learn a great deal about it, but when he turned back to the men he discovered that they had long been speaking in exactly the same tone of voice about other things, about art and things like that. He saw all at once that their enthusiasm was nothing but vehemence, and that they had nothing in common except their fantasies. He drew back from them. He stayed home again in the evenings, devoted himself with greater diligence to his studies at the university, and imagined for a while that everything was as it had been. Until on one such evening as that when he'd found Luisa in the kitchen with her ghosts, his most private meditations formed themselves, completely out of the blue, into words. Since then, too, he had known that he looked into the eyes of people on the street differently, straining to find in their expressions the traces of that suffering with which his nation was supposed to be visited. Here and there he now believed he really noticed an oppressed, enslaved figure, but when he looked closer he realized with disappointment that it was only the burden of poverty or of wretchedness that lay on the stranger's shoulders, not the yoke of slavery. And yet it would not let him rest. He still sensed powers within himself and enquired every day whether his nation had need of them. He became ever more perplexed and dissatisfied, he could stand neither to be in the lecture hall nor in the living room where Luisa sat and waited for him with great, questioning eyes. So he went on long walks.

Once in springtime he'd been walking along the Pod-skali,[10] deep in thought, and when he looked up, a square,

---

10. Podskalí, meaning "under the cliff," was a district to the north of

gray building loomed in front of him on partially excavated ground, its windows staring at him emptily, as if burned out. Wanka took it for a former barracks that had now been given over to demolition, and, as the place didn't seem otherwise fenced off, he entered through one of the yawning gates. The courtyards were filled with door frames and doors, planks and all sorts of old clutter, and these objects looked unbelievably gloomy in the lusterless, slow-fading light of the late afternoon. The student turned away and, directed by some sort of feeling, climbed the trodden-down wooden stairs and walked along wide, white corridors and through many whitewashed rooms that had low ceilings and partially torn-up tiles. Then he mounted one more flight of stairs and again found himself in a corridor of which the end wall was already half torn down, so that the wind could enter abundantly out of the gray day. It tore straws loose from the rafters in the ceiling and drove them like arrows toward the intruder. Wanka entered at one of the very next doors and found himself in a narrow cell, barely three paces wide and not much longer, very evenly filled with the sparse light that flowed in through a barred opening near the ceiling. The gray-white walls were covered with many scratches as if to form a strange, confused pattern, and it took a moment for the student to realize that this pattern resolved itself into words and pictures. He read prayers and curses, names and places, and everything was scratched into wild, grinning caricatures, remarkably fused with the lines of their noses and eyes, more like eloquent folds and wrinkles than like written characters. One face grew out from behind the other, pale and palpitating; like a mass of people the ever more awakening wall pressed toward him, at the very front a threatening, furious man with hollow eyes. Straight across his forehead stood "Jesus Mary."

Vyšehrad. In 1893 major clearing operations were undertaken here and in other areas of the inner city to ameliorate the unhygenic and outdated housing conditions.

Then Wanka heard someone speak his name, and in indescribable horror he turned as if to flee and bumped violently into Rezek, the pale student, who said with a characteristic and conspiratorial smile, "These were artists too, these here, weren't they?"

Wanka recognized the student and stared uncomprehendingly at him.

"Well, I mean, each in his own way," he still smiled. Then he added solemnly, "Believe me, these pictures touch me more than what our painters paint and our poets rhyme up. Do you know what this is? Folk songs. Not composed a thousand years ago and not incomprehensible after ten thousand years. Poems in an eternal language. They should remove these walls just as carefully as the walls of hieroglyphs in the pyramids. They should hang them in the churches, because they're sacred. Look here," and he laid his thin, hard finger on a drawing which, with awkward lines, represented a small house, "Desire made this, and Faith wrote a prayer underneath it and Despair a curse, and Mockery drew a caricature around it all with sore, bleeding nails, in which the dear little house looks like a greedy, wide-open maw. Have you ever seen a more terrible painting?"

"Come on," said Wanka, gripped by sudden terror.

Rezek followed. "I come here often," he said. "The demolition work is going so slowly. I read from these walls as from the Book of Revelation. I've found the answer to many questions there."

They were silent. "Of course," Rezek added as they passed through the gate, "the answer is ultimately another question. But only one, always the same one, and that's not as dreadful as the many."

"What kind of building is that, anyway?" Wanka now asked, turning back toward the abandoned hulk that stood black and huge with its empty windows before the evening.

Rezek looked up. "The old St. Wenceslas Penitentiary."

He paused to light a cigarette. Then they walked in silence toward the city.

The two young men, who had often passed by each other before, now met nearly every day. But it was more a power over his will than his own intention that drew Wanka to his somber colleague; and what then held him there was the fact that Rezek guessed all the questions that had tortured him in the last while and answered the unuttered ones as if by instinct. Of course Zdenko didn't see how far these answers projected beyond his questions, and so it came about that his strength and the naive intelligence of his chaste youth soon stood blindly in the service of the energetic agitator, to whom they must have been very opportune and advantageous. The increased strictness of the police force, the affair of "King Bohush" and other semipolitical incidents, had rendered the young people cautious and uneasy, and for some of his ends Rezek had to make use of the mercenary rabble, who then acted as informers against him at the first opportunity. But this was the dream of the shady man: to find uncorrupted young people of good background who, convinced of the justice of their undertaking, would strive toward a national liberation with the whole blind brute strength of their dispositions, and pursue with youthful undauntedness a goal in which he himself was not always willing to believe.

On their shared walks, in which Luisa took an auditor's part, they had discovered a small, unfrequented pub high up on the Hradčany. From its round alcove they often watched how the heavy, somber spring evenings ravaged the city, how their fire tore at the cupolas and towers and here and there flashed like madness out of the brooding eyes of two windows. And the whole weight of these ominous twilights lay on the three young people. Then the energetic Rezek, who had a great fear of these still, wide hours, would inevitably turn to the pensive girl and say with a hard voice,

"Loisinka, play something for us." And out of the niche where Luisa was sitting the lingering tones of a harmonium would rustle like the beating of wings, and the simple folk songs made the young people still more quiet and lonesome. It grew darker and darker around them, and they must have seemed to themselves like leave-takers who wave good-bye and yet can't recognize one another anymore . . . Until the song broke off in the middle of a note and the tremulous fading of the harmonium blended with the timid sobs that broke out in Luisa. Then Rezek ordered: "Do play something cheerful . . ."

But Luisa only knew a few folk songs, and her brother said: "Our nation doesn't have any happy notes. Its favorite songs are as if before weeping."

Then Rezek began to pace up and down in the small room with vigorous strides, and finally he stopped in the alcove and said:

"Our nation is like a child. Sometimes I see it clearly: our hatred for the Germans isn't really anything political, but something — how shall I put it? — something human. Our grudge is not that we have to share our homeland with the Germans, but that we're growing up among such a mature race — that makes us sad. It's the story of the child who grows up among old people. It learns to smile before it has ever known how to laugh."

But when the waitress had lit the lamp, Rezek sat down in the large old armchair and, with his yellow, nervous hands pressed in front of his eyes, began to speak as if to himself: "What use is it all. When the people were told, 'You are young,' the educated ones were ashamed of it. And they quickly grew old, instead of growing older. Instead of enjoying each day, they had to have a yesterday and a day before yesterday. The Königinhofer manuscript, to be sure![11] Not

---

11. A manuscript containing ancient Czech poems from the thirteenth century, which Václav Hanka claimed to have discovered in 1817 in Königinhof

satisfied with that, they looked for their culture among foreigners and indeed there where it is the readiest — among the French. And so it happened that there are centuries between the educated Czechs and the people. They don't understand one another any more. We have only old men and children, so far as culture is concerned. We have our beginning and our end at the same time. We can't last. *That* is our tragedy, not the Germans."

Luisa saw the alarm that impressed itself on her brother's features during this confession. He seemed to hold himself back with difficulty, all his sinews tensed as if to spring.

Rezek no longer noticed it. It was as if he had awakened from a bad dream, and the stern accent in his voice seemed to recall everything that had gone before. That evening he developed the most daring plans and, with his characteristic shrewdness, inquired so relentlessly into all methods and possibilities, he seemed so sure of himself about the aims of his tireless agitation, that Zdenko was once again completely submerged in his influence.

Nevertheless, this evening represented for Wanka the beginning of a fierce internal struggle. He had felt proud and strong in his mission so long as he believed he was exerting himself on behalf of a young and healthy nation, and now he had discovered that this nation suffered from internal dissension and despaired even of itself. And he lost all his joy and all his courage. He was like the reckless lieutenant who hurls himself, at the head of his troops, into the superior forces of the enemy. He realizes that the defeat of his side is already sealed, and what a moment before was still a joyous act of heroism is a useless, despairing sacrifice to him. The poor youth all at once feels so much that is new and undissipated and lonesome in himself, that refuses to

---

on the Elbe, a town in northeastern Bohemia. A long and passionate argument ensued over the authenticity of the manuscript, and it was eventually exposed as a forgery.

come to an end and longs to blossom in another quiet spring.

The high and bright words of national enthusiasm had faded for him, and more than once Wanka plunged out of the fervent, furtive meetings into the nighttime streets, through which he wandered aimlessly toward an uncertain morning. But so strong a hold did Rezek's personality exert over him that, in the midst of his broodings, he always looked to him for a way out and didn't dare to confess his growing doubts to his shady companion. He didn't talk about it to anyone. He noticed the anxious question in the eyes of his simple mother and thought to drown it out with his vehement, hasty tenderness. He inclined more intimately toward his pale little sister, and it was as if he were trying to find himself again in these fleeting moments of a pure love.

Now Luisa began apprehensively to understand the strife in Zdenko's soul. She knew nothing of the incipient disloyalty toward his task, and that he felt the duty he had assumed to be a coercion. But she saw that he was tearing at some sort of chain, and that seemed to her to be the iron power of Rezek, from which he escaped only to return again and again, weak and despairing. For a long time the figure of that pallid man had been standing over her as well. She found his image in all her thoughts and was no longer surprised by it. It seemed to her that he belonged there like the Crucified One in a cloister cell. And she couldn't prevent him from growing into her dreams as well, and from finally becoming one with the dark prince in the old dream of the masquerade and so no longer known to her as Rezek, but as Julius Caesar. And then something odd happened to the girl. Some scenes out of distant years, and half-forgotten dreams, and figures, and strange, crimson words that she had heard from her brother, and other things that she wasn't even able to explain, crowded around her like a new, fantastical time in which every law is altered, and every duty. She could no longer distinguish between doing and dreaming, and viewed all everyday events in the colors of that bloody ball at Krumlov, the deepest and most disturbing of her memories. She now lived amid the still, festive figures and felt more and more clearly that she too must have a role in this secret dance. And for days she would sit by the window, a forgotten piece of work in her lap, gazing with lost eyes at the high, bare walls of the Maltese church and pondering: What can it be, what?

The lazy, sluggish summer days went slowly on toward the feast of the Assumption of the Blessed Virgin.[12] A heavy gloom hung over the Wanka household. The homesickness that the four individuals had already almost forgotten came over them again in a different, unexpected form. They no longer yearned for the past; instead they dreamed, in the hot rooms behind thickly curtained windows, of the light, breezy village summer, to which the cool woods are so near a neighbor. Of the bright country lanes over which the young fruit trees spread their shadows, touchingly thin, so that one moves along them as on a ladder, from line to line. Of the heavy, ripe fields that begin to wave so broadly and splendidly toward evening, and of the groves where silent ponds lie in their darkling stillness, deeper than anyone can guess. And then each of the four individuals would think of some specific, trivial hour, whose dainty happiness he just happened to carry off with him without knowing its value. This longing was all the more painful in that it did not apply to something irrecoverable, in that each of them felt how the happy summer of home awaited him and how it grew sad when no one came. So as to be nearer to it, at least, they made little excursions along the Vltava, and the forester's widow believed most readily the benevolent rural lies of the little woods behind Kuchelbad,[13] and she was filled

---

12. August 15.
13. Kuchelbad, or Malá Chuchle, originally a rural area on the west bank of the Vltava, south of the city, now belongs to the fifth district of Prague.

with that unconscious gladness which belongs to older, in-
dustrious people. She was quiet and meditative; though she
hardly smiled, the folds around her lips had disappeared,
and this brought into her face something young and sunny
that she had perhaps never possessed as a bride. Then also
she hardly noticed how seldom Zdenko lifted his gaze from
the knotty path into the light landscape, and how quickly
the summer flowers wilted in Luisa's hot hands. Old Rosalka
stayed home completely and sulked. She said of the summer,
No, if it won't come to me I'm not going to run after it;
and, sitting down at the kitchen window with an old prayer
book, she fell asleep over her piety.

There was only one whom the dusty August days didn't
seem to weigh down: Rezek. His strength remained tireless;
most recently there was even a boisterous merriment in his
character that Wanka could not comprehend. He didn't
know that Rezek always became so uncontrolled when danger rose up close behind him and his secret efforts, and he
interpreted this change rather as a sign of success.

His last reservations vanished when, in the course of a
walk that the three of them were taking according to their
old habit, Rezek proposed that they stop at the Vikárka (a
small, ancient pub across from St. Vitus's Cathedral). They
sat at a dark table in the innermost room and toasted with
genuine Melnik.[14] The student wasn't stingy with the wine,
and his merriment grew so noisy that the few remaining
guests — they were bishop's lackeys — had to share in it.
Rezek narrated the legend of the Bread Countess, who was
thought to wander about in the old Czernin Palace[15]; he
attached his spiteful mockery to the most suspenseful parts,

14. A renowned wine produced in the region of Mělník, a town in northern
Bohemia where the Elbe and the Vltava converge.
15. The baroque Černín Palace on Loretto Square (Loretánské náměstí), a
square on Hradčany, was built between 1703 and 1726 by the Italian architect
Francesco Caratti. The largest palace in Prague, it now houses the Ministry of
Foreign Affairs.

thus altering the effect of his words in a strange and surprising manner. Here and there other stories awoke (they lurk in every corner of these shadowy rooms) and it came about that Zdenko obliged with the legends of Krumlov, including the one about Julius Caesar.

"Actually that would be your business," he had said first to Luisa.

But she only shook her head mutely, then lifted her wine glass and held it to her lips for a long time. She began to suck at it, keeping her mouth nearly closed, while her eyes stared hugely into the liquid, the crimson reflection spreading over her narrow little face.

All at once Rezek said, "The way you tell that. Remarkable. Isn't there a resemblance between our time and the days before the Thirty Years' War?"

Something quivered beneath his words. Zdenko and others laughed. But Luisa lifted the beaker slowly from her cool red mouth and looked up at the student with frightened eyes.

Later, when they were on their way home, Rezek stopped near the old castle steps in front of a gate where a black coat of arms gleamed proudly over the arch, and asked: "Have you ever been inside?"

The siblings said no.

"So you don't even know the Daliborka?[16] Shame on you."

Already Rezek was entering through the narrow door frame of the gate, and Luisa, who stood beside him, saw a neat courtyard where the wide, warm afternoon shadows couched, watched over by the bright walls. A little old woman came out of the door of the house with greetings,

---

16. A prison tower on the east side of Hradčany, constructed in 1496 and named after the knight Dalibor of Kozojedy, the first prisoner to be executed there for giving refuge to rebellious peasants. The popular legend that Dalibor played the violin to cheer himself and charm his jailor is based on a double-entendre, since the instrument of torture was popularly called a "violin."

shooed a flock of hens away in front of her, and then waved to the strangers to follow. Zdenko went first, then came Rezek and finally Luisa, for the path was so narrow that they had to walk one behind the other. Luisa hesitated a bit and looked around with glistening eyes: there was a ridiculously tiny vegetable garden; a six-year-old child could surely have counted its cabbages and asparagus stalks. Right in the middle, though, towered a sturdy apple tree, which seemed to display its small red fruits to the city that shimmered away in the distance. A few densely overgrown steps led downward to a damp and dusky part of the slope, and there stood many wild rose bushes whose branches were reluctant to let Luisa pass. Rezek stopped, and the girl heard Zdenko's voice: "So this is the famous Hunger Tower. In there the Knight Dalibor learned, out of longing, to play the violin. That was here, wasn't it?"

"Yes," Rezek replied, "but I always think he'd known violin playing before. Longing seldom sings."

And then they were already standing in front of the heavily studded door of the gray tower. Luisa looked up and noticed that the thick walls were only partially covered by a newly constructed roof. At the open edge of the battlement a slim young acacia rose up at the side of a bedraggled silver thistle, lifting its pallid leaf clusters with delicate charm into the bright sky. That was the last image of day. It grew steadily damper and blacker, and the musty air spread itself like a veil in front of the girl's eyes. "Can she find her way after us?" she heard the student ask. He held out his hand to her. His voice emerged rough and unfamiliar out of the uncertain depths of the vault, and Luisa was in no condition to answer. She felt her way along the icy walls with bated breath, shivering quietly, and only came to herself again when the reddish glow of a light approached her out of the next chamber, as if to warm her. There she found the two men and the woman in the middle of the room leaning over something, and a smouldering candle swayed at the end of a cord directly above their lowered heads. Then the light slid lower and lower with a screeching sound past the three faces, which were lit up harshly for a second; it sank as far as their feet and vanished slowly into a black, round opening in the ground, over which a last dying glow twitched back and forth. Then Luisa leaned forward as well and made out how the candle, tiny, arrived far below in a second gray chamber, under which still a third, black, seemed to begin.

"Oh," said Luisa.

Zdenko grasped her moist, trembling hand: "Be careful, Luisa."

And then the old woman related something in a weak, monotonous voice, which seemed to dread the damp walls and whirred in timid circles close about the four heads. "The new ones," she was just saying, quietly and secretively, as if this were a dear, personal remembrance that she was entrusting to someone for the first time, "the new ones who came down here received a piece of bread and a pitcher of water. Yes, and they had to sustain themselves on the bread and the water, and they had to sit there at the hole and watch as the one who'd already been sitting down there a week or two, well, depending (some people have so much stubborn strength), slowly starved to death. Well, and then, when in God's name it was over, then they were let down . . ."

"On this cord?" teased Zdenko.

The woman didn't allow herself to be interrupted. "They were let down and first they had to shove the dead man, the one they watched die of starvation, into the hole in the ground there — look." (They all leaned forward.)

"Sometimes they must have half gobbled up their predecessor," Rezek laughed gruesomely.

"Might well be," the old woman murmured and then went on with her long-accustomed explanation.

Luisa leaned against her brother. "It's deep?" she inquired.

"Very deep."

"And can no one get back out?"

"No," Rezek now explained. "The thing is like a bottle, narrow at the top and hollowed out wider and wider toward its base. You'd hardly be able to climb back. Incidentally, that would be the best cure for surfeited people even today."

Luisa heard him laugh. The concierge pulled the candle halfway up and then stepped further back into the room. The men followed her. Now the fleeting, timid glow of a match here and there opened up unguessed niches and corridors, which seemed in the next instant to collapse again soundlessly. An uncertain shuffling began. The light over the crater grew nervous, and the broad darkness all around seemed to awaken, to expand and to stream past Luisa in growing shapes. Ever more clearly she recognized couple after couple. They took their places for a reeling dance, and out of the circling and swaying He finally came toward her astonished eyes: Julius Caesar.

He was mute and black. Her heart pounded up into her throat and, alarmed, she dropped her gaze and he fell, fell down into a limitless depth. She knew — she was standing at the edge of the tower. So she was herself the young lady in blue. By her shivering she felt that she was without clothes, totally without clothes. With trembling fingers she felt along her body and perceived its naked smoothness. Then she looked up: above her was night, starless. And then he stood beside her, almost in front of her, near the abyss. The young lady in blue took her revenge: this time it was his turn. And she raised her hands instinctively and thrust them directly toward him, until they pressed at his shoulders — but then, in the moment of the sudden contact, she grasped him convulsively, snatched him back, toward herself, felt him, and in a new, deep, trembling bliss, her senses left her.

In the end it seemed it was indeed the sullen Rosalka, who found Zdenko's efforts and his mother's ambitious wish arrogant and sinful, who would be proved right. For it must have been something like arrogance that moved the young man to change his residence three times within three weeks; that is, out of the little bedroom that looked out on the Maltese walls, into detention pending trial, from there into the hospital and then at last to the Seventh Cemetery of Olshany,[17] where his mother bought a plot of land for him, three paces in length and two wide. He wanted no more. All this had happened so quickly that the woman with her aging intellect could not find her way at all into this unexpected, sudden rise in status, could only shake her head, and was perpetually on her way to the strange, tiny landholding, as if she couldn't comprehend that the new owner was happy out there. She forgot about work and food and returned every third day to the hospital doctor, who finally wearied of explaining to the disturbed mother again and again the tragic case of pneumonia with fatal consequences, and adding that with such infamous autumn weather it was not to be wondered at. Then, when Mrs. Wanka, having been virtually pushed out the door by the impatient doctor and the waiting visitors, stepped out into the pearl-gray-gloomy drizzling day, she resolved every time to take a really close look at the weather in order to arrive at an understanding of the "tragic case." Once outside, though, she hurried timidly past the houses and the people, and, breathless, reached her apartment, where she found Luisa, always in the same spot, with hot, dry eyes and feverish hands. Then they remained seated opposite each other, without lighting the lamp, without saying anything, very far apart, until it was so dark that they forgot about one another. From time to time one of the women got up and went on tiptoe, as if

17. The Olšany cemetery in Žižkov was created in 1680 as the burial ground for victims of the plague; since 1782 it has been Prague's main cemetery. It contains both the grave of Rudolf Mrva, the historical "King Bohush," and the family grave of the Rilkes (located at section 8, number 43). R. M. Rilke himself is buried in Switzerland.

to keep the other from noticing, into Zdenko's long-abandoned, dusty little bedroom. She entered cautiously. And only when she found the empty desk and the neglected, covered bed did the mad smile of a wild, ever-credulous hope die on her twitching lips. But then the one who was left behind listened; she heard the door fall to. And then weeping, frightened and hopeless, began in the abandoned chamber. Until one Saturday old Rosalka cleaned up the small back room and then took the key into her possession. But the weeping didn't stop; during the day it filled up both the rooms, and every night it seemed to wander searchingly through the whole building, so that the children could not sleep. Even adults kept a light burning until morning, for everyone in the old house wanted to keep an eye on the corners of his room and was secretly glad when the next gray, rainy day beat against the panes. To those who complained about it, the maid Rosalka swore by her soul and her honor that there was nothing to be done about it except setting up holy water and saying an Our Father; for thus it happened every time someone died with many worldly wishes in his heart and without the proper rest and resignation. So they prayed while peeling turnips and while washing dishes, the neighbors prayed, and the peddler-woman under the arcades prayed too. And they sprinkled holy water after the two women who approached through the hall and the corridors with those slow, rhythmic steps that they had learned at the rear of the hearse. Mrs. Wanka often went out and hurried along a few streets, only to come aimlessly back home. But Luisa didn't stir from her place. She no longer had any fantasies, and in her dreams all the colors had grown as pale as the days outside. Sometimes she counted the drops on the windows and listened: something roared past her like a great river in which many broken, incomprehensible words drifted, always more and more — and she thought, it's like after a flood. Then she suddenly started up, as if someone had called her, and — began once more to count the many trickling drops.

All Souls' Day arrived. At that time even the broad streets of the New Town seem lost in thought. In the elegant flower shops rich, showy wreaths lie ready, and the strange blossoms in them are incapable of smiling. The entertainment sections of the advertising pillars are pasted over with blank paper; only the state theater announced the performance of the old churchyard comedy *The Miller and His Child,*[18] and in the display windows of the art galleries three, four, five dim photographs have been pushed in front of the colorful English prints, illustrations of the quiet, melancholy song by Hermann von Gilm: "Set the sweet-smelling mignonettes on the table. . . ."[19] On the moistly glistening "Moat" the lanterns are lit early, and still cabs and hackney carriages drive by with large palm wreaths on coachman's seat and carriage roof, and on the occasional tram a pine bough or even a metal wreath is hung over the colored lantern at the rear; not for the first time must it survive this journey on the day of the dead. Over the unsympathetic Žižkov[20] the arched lamps with their unbelievably long necks have already risen like many melancholy moons, and beneath them, before the gates of the ever-expanding cemetery, there is an unfestive press of people: of cried-out people, who, a few half-wilted cut flowers in their hands, throng toward their goal with dark longing; of enraged people, who don't understand the urgency of grief; of nonparticipating, celebrating, laughing, and watching people, and many others.

18. *Der Müller und sein Kind,* a sentimental folk drama written in 1835 by E. B. S. Raupach (1784–1852).

19. The first line of the poem "Allerseelen" ("All Souls' ") by the Austrian poet Hermann von Gilm (1812–1864).

20. An eastern district of Prague located at the foot of Vítkov hill, renamed Žižkov after the Hussite general Jan Žižka, who won a monumental victory there in 1420. Žižkov was largely constructed in the midnineteenth century as a lower-class residential suburb, and it became a town in 1881.

The paths are narrowed by the brash, lurking vendors' stalls, and the children in the long train attach themselves like fishhooks to the lamps and gingerbread and playthings on display, so that new traffic jams keep occurring. But with the crowd and over it that dense heavy haze of sad, tiredly fragrant blossoms, wilted leaves, rain-soaked earth, and damp clothes, in which words seem to stick, wallows toward the wide, luminous garden. There the masses do separate into the individual avenues, but actually none but a very few are making an effort to arrive quickly at the grave where they intend to leave a gift. First they want to have seen the other blessed dead in their holiday garb, and they find it too entertaining to stroll over to the stone vaults of the distinguished, to read the long unfamiliar names, and to take pleasure in the flowers which completely cover the costly marble. Then to gawk inside the dusky burial chapels with the bright, shining altars, before which a weathered old grandmother is already exerting herself for the second day to make the memorialized ones, who are total strangers to her, comprehend the well-paid Our Fathers and Hail Marys of the remaining family members. And from this contemplation of light and luster an unconscious, lively gladness creeps into the faces of the crowd, which contrasts strangely with the few wounded, shadowy figures who, timid and black, press along the edge of the path. In blind impatience they here and there push a happy spectator to the side, and he sends a thought after them: Birds of death, what are they doing here?

In the Seventh Cemetery it is somewhat more open and solitary. There is more space here, for only a part of the fenced-in land is filled with graves and tombs; beyond this there is unsuspecting, healthy, well-watered ground, which retains the traces of its former harvests and which has painlessly produced, out of its now-superfluous potency, a lush, wild, mindless garden. This was a good neighborhood for poor Zdenko Wanka, who still bounded the row of graves along the left wall, as if no one had dared to die since then in the great city with its many abysses. The two abandoned women, mother and daughter, were already keeping him company for the second day, and old Rosalka came now and then and talked to the deaf sorrow of these two about the splendor and the luster of other tombs. That Zdenko's mound refused to become really festive, despite the many gillyflowers, asters, and forget-me-nots, was because through all the ornamentation somewhere the wet, new ground always penetrated, in which the grass seed had not yet had time to sprout. The fresh grave seemed to hang back a bit timidly, like someone who finds himself for the first time in a company whose ways and manners he is not yet familiar with. Nor were the two visitors able yet to really find the language of communication with the lost one, and so the dead Zdenko's first holiday must have been quite gloomy. Mrs. Josephine no longer cried. She sat on a little wooden bench of the kind that are to be found at the foot of the graves, and she had surely forgotten that the damp, apathetic autumn evening was sinking down ever more densely about her. The daughter, who looked even smaller and paler than usual in her little black cashmere dress, was watching, without really knowing it, the scene that was taking place at a grave opposite them. A thin, careworn man had just laid down a little blue lamp and a posy of lilies of the valley on the mound, and there had been a timorous, moving tenderness in his gesture, something of that unaided charm of young people in love. But when he stood up again and pressed his crying three-year-old child to his black, poorly cut Sunday suit, this gesture was broken off curtly, and a trembling, hopeless sorrow began to weigh him down. He fought against it, and again and again he sought the eyes of the child, perhaps to recall what the mother's eyes were like, or to draw a little luster and hope from them. But the child was crying . . .

Then a group of black-garbed young men in the national dress, the *czamara*,[21] intruded between Luisa and those two motherless ones. They were, for the most part, students, friends and companions of Wanka, who came on this day to the graves of their heroes and companions with political orations and songs, to lift them above the law of equality that ruled within these still walls. The opposition that was leveled anew each year against their enterprise by the cautious authorities was to blame for the fact that these announcements took on a loud, ostentatious character, beyond all sincerity, and that the youthful boisterousness wouldn't content itself with the quiet laying-down of its blossoming love. So now, too, the rows formed to strike up one of the stern battle songs at Wanka's grave, to remind him who had made his peace with everything of the days of tempest. After all, the loyal comrade — and Wanka had died in loyalty — must be pleased to hear of the perseverance of his brothers; he must, as it were, step among them again for a moment when his own words and wishes awoke over his grave mound. Only when the signal to begin was about to be given, the young people drew apart with dull murmurs. They were suddenly ashamed to shout their rough resistance song into the deep, sacred grief of these black women, and the best of them had an intuition of eternity. They lowered the large wreath, with cards bearing their names stuck into its evergreen, at the very end of the grave, as if they perceived uncertainly that he who had traveled hand in hand with them up to this spot no longer fully belonged to them after all, at least not in his most private longing.

From their number Rezek stayed behind. Solemn and tall, arms crossed in front of his breast, he stood there and only cast down his pale, hard face as if in meditation. Perhaps he was the only one who guessed that Zdenko had died of

21. A *čamara*, from the Spanish *zamarra*, sheep's fleece, was a uniformlike jacket worn by Slavic patriots.

ruined happiness, even if he himself could least of all understand it. His was a stern Savonarola nature, which here and there in the country set fire to heaps of kindling, and young, credulous people came, who laid all their riches in the flames: happiness and laughter and desire. For the fanatic wanted an impoverished and renouncing army behind him, because he knew that there is no wilder weapon than despair. And his law found adherents even in this soft, Slavic race, which loses and denies itself with the treasures of its own spirit.

Luisa, too, had timidly laid down before him all that was left to her from her dream-dark childhood; he hadn't noticed it, for she didn't seem to him to be a comrade whose acquisition would be of value. And then Luisa had added something else to her offering, something unclear, painfully blissful, for which she had no name; but Rezek hadn't recognized it, because it was her first, trembling love.

As he now stepped closer to the girl, he felt, perhaps for the first time, that he wasn't bending over a child, and involuntarily his eye saluted the woman. But Luisa didn't understand him; he was far from her, passed away like everything else. He was barely a memory to her. And so his eye took leave of her in the same instant, and he bowed deeply, as Luisa had never seen him do, and left. It was already almost night, and Luisa couldn't follow him with her hurting eyes beyond the next crosses.

The night after this All Souls' Day there was no weeping in the house across from the Maltese church. Even before it was quite light, Mrs. Josephine got up, dressed herself more painstakingly than usual and informed her daughter that today, since she had missed so many Mondays, she was going to the Colonel's. Luisa looked up with weak surprise. Her mother's voice seemed completely foreign to her as she now added that she certainly had no intention of losing that good and aristocratic household. She would also be pleased if Luisa would come to pick her up, to put the Meerings in memory of her. Then Mrs. Wanka left. The whole house gazed like a single stony astonishment after her steps, which showed almost exactly the same energetic vigor that she had commanded before the tragedy. There was indeed something surprising and uncanny about this hasty, jerking self-resurrection after weeks of the most unsteady abandon. During the two days at her son's grave Mrs. Josephine must have discovered within herself some reserve of strength and energy, the existence of which she had forgotten about for several years. That she certainly knew how to apply it is shown by the fact that Mrs. von Meering could describe the grief of the mother as not deep and heartfelt enough. Expecting to see a broken woman, she found her almost stiff with standing upright: she'd been so ready and willing to be moved and feeling-filled in the face of eloquent grief, and now she saw something that might at best be called silent mourning, toward which she felt a strong, uncomfortable embarrassment. Added to this was the curiosity to learn from this most reliable source how much of "what they say" was true. The Colonel had brought home very peculiar rumors from the table of regulars at the Pike, where there was plenty of blathering on about politics, stories in which all the political slogans of recent time came up, in such a light, in fact, that it suddenly seemed dubious to Mr. von Meering and his wife to entertain members of such a suspicious Czech family in their house, and a solemn family council was held, in which pro and con, justly weighed, produced no real resolution. The death of the youth who had gone astray rendered the old military man somewhat more lenient, and what finally settled matters was the clever reflection that first of all only the mother, who was to all intents and purposes the respectable widow of a royal gamekeeper, had access to the Meering von Meerhelm residence, and that the above-mentioned capable widow came into close contact only with the fine linen, which was, moreover, for its part, since it

came from Rumburg,[22] proof against Czechification, and by
virtue of the noble five-pointed crown monogram, belong-
ing (for ten years now) to the von Meerhelms, was also
proof against all democratic influences. So it came about
that Mrs. Josephine found a very friendly reception, and it
went without saying that the old Monday washdays would
from then on again be honored. Mrs. von Meering didn't
relinquish her quiet conviction that on some future occasion
she might learn more details; that this hadn't already happened at the first reunion she took as an insult, and she
could not resist assuring the widow, in the most innocent
tones, of her profound empathy with the misfortune, "which
was so much more painful still because of its interesting
circumstances." This comment, which let her appear informed and aware, impressed her greatly, and she held it for
a fine attack on the "ungrateful taciturnity of these people."

Mrs. Wanka, however, hadn't noticed anything at all,
neither of the disappointment of the colonel's wife, nor of
the blow with which she took her revenge. She had quite a
few things to mull over in her own mind these days, and
the consequences of her pensiveness now came to life, blow
for blow, in rapid succession. First a small notice appeared
in one Bohemian and one German daily paper, which assured a respectable young man of a quiet, well-furnished
room in a tranquil neighborhood, and whoever tracked
down this promise would suddenly have found himself in
the Lesser Town, would have asked the peddler-woman
under the arcades for "Number 87 new," and received the
broad, detailed answer that it was three flights up at Wankas
and that Wankas now wished to sublet to gentlemen, probably because they'd really had such an incredible amount of
bad luck. Now depending on whether the young, respectable
man is more young or more respectable, he may hear much

22. A town on the northern border of Bohemia with a large textile industry,
which had 10,000 German inhabitants in 1899.

or little about the fate of the gamekeeper's family here in the listening, gossipy darkness of the arcades. It is uncertain to what extent Ernst Land was instructed when, one November day, he came in danger twice of breaking neck and legs on the familiar winding staircase of "87 new" and, after various doors had been slammed shut in indignation at his German inquiry, finally stood in front of old Rosalka, who regarded him with great mistrust. She didn't like him, she knew that in an instant. He was "too German" for her. Now and again she felt this way toward a person, although she didn't know what called the impression forth — hardly knew if it was an excess or a lack. She stared into the lenses of his fogged-up pince-nez, failed to find the eyes behind it, and had the German question repeated to her twice, even though she had understood it. It only appeased her a little when the young gentleman, in very strange Bohemian and with great exertion, told the story of a room which was supposed to be to let somewhere. For five days Land had been repeating this claim before all sorts of doors, and he was perfectly fed up and tired of the cooking odors and maledictions that he had received for his pains. Since Mrs. Wanka, with whom he could communicate in German, didn't make any disproportionate demands, and the back room seemed to him quiet and acceptable, he decided to stay. "I don't make any noise," he said in his rather anxious voice at the end of their conversation, "and you won't be bothered by me. During the day I'm at work a lot, and in the evenings — God, then one reads a bit and . . ." "Please, please," replied Mrs. Wanka, also somewhat embarrassed. And in the doorway she turned back a little: "Pardon me, sir, perhaps I may inquire what you are?" A pause.

"A pharmacist," the young man said sadly as he stared into the walls of the Maltese church.

They really didn't bother each other, the Wankas and the young chemist's assistant. They hardly saw each other. Luisa avoided meeting him; it was too painful to her to see a strange person enter Zdenko's room, and she couldn't comprehend how her mother could have brought herself to do it. She didn't understand her mother at all any more, since she had had a long talk with her one evening, much of which was on the subject of eternal idleness, more still on duty and work. And when Luisa timidly declared herself ready to go into service or work in a shop, something very astonishing happened. "You have to look higher up, that's not for you" — this was approximately the widow's reply — "I should have thought of it right at the beginning. What did you take piano lessons for in Krumlov — you got on quite well with that. And in French. If you hadn't neglected it after our move to Prague, you'd already be able to give lessons by now."

Luisa listened: "Give lessons?"

"Of course. Just recently Mrs. Colonel said to me she'd know of a nice position for you, if you only knew a bit about managing children, and the rudiments of French . . ." Luisa didn't even hear the rest; what her mother was saying was too new and strange to her. But often in the evenings, when her mother was settling accounts with Rosalka in the kitchen, and Luisa, already half undressed, sat the edge of her bed and felt so very tired and small, she folded her hands and recited her first child's prayer and believed its dear, faded words — that she was really still a child, a small, blonde child, and she longed to have something over her like a snug, trusty shelter, and then she dreamed of angels with wide golden wings.

But, despite all that, things really happened according to her mother's intention. Luisa took lessons in music and French, several hours a day, and her teachers gave assurances that she was making good progress. She herself was unaware of it. She gradually realized that she had once possessed other splendid, fairy-tale things — it was a long time ago — and that the substitute she was now being given was poor and cold and lacked all beauty. She lived through one winter in numb, docile resignation, without anything changing except that she grew paler, smaller, and more quiet. Her steps could barely be heard any more, and how often one of the neighbors' children took fright when, without the stairs having creaked, she stood in the middle of the corridor, and it usually ran away screaming when the girl held her pallid hands toward it with timid tenderness.

So on the surface these seemed to be very quiet times, in which everyone did his duty without excitement or interruption; and yet a still and inexorable struggle went on between the competent, active widow, who grew more vigorous every day, and the suffering girl, who in her amazement still didn't know what was happening to her, and couldn't find any other weapon against her mother's relentless decisiveness than this imperceptible mute wilting, which imparted such a moving, melancholy beauty to her little face.

Perhaps Ernst Land saw this beauty, but he didn't recognize it. He was afraid of the women, and yet some evenings he thought of them, of some indefinite image of charm and kindness, which sometimes held its tending hands over him and sometimes depended, anxious and timid, on his protection and his help. He had grown up in poor conditions in the middle of the city, without siblings, without friends, practically forced into growing up by his old, embittered father who couldn't wait for the son to begin earning a living. He finally tore him away from his studies just as the youth had begun to take pleasure in science, and considered his duty done from the moment when Ernst was taken on and provided for in a pharmacy. Now he could do what he liked. "Now the world has opened its doors to you," the elder Land was in the habit of declaring with the utmost pathos of which he was capable. But the young man didn't seem to have any longing after this "open world." His thoughts made no pilgrimages out into the new and the unknown; when he didn't watch them, they returned

by a thousand secret paths to the one extinguished loveliness
of his childhood and knelt down before a small, melancholy
woman, of whom he knew nothing except that she sang soft
Slavic songs and that, at the time when he began to go to
school, she lay in the dark back room on the bed and, without telling anyone about it, very slowly and soundlessly, for
the length of about a year, died. At that time he was almost
afraid of her, but when she'd gone away so soon he missed
her everywhere, and fell into the habit of always attributing
everything good that happened to him to her tender love,
which he believed was still watching over his days. This
happens to children orphaned at an early age. They refuse
to touch all the joys that their playmates carelessly and bliss-
fully share among themselves, but wind them always in still
faithfulness about the one dark image of their longing,
which, in this frame of touching sacrifices, gradually appears
clearer, happier, more interested. And because they remain
poor, they remain alone, and because they don't tell their
joys, they don't win any companions for them. As a rule,
he whose mother has not shown him the way into the world
seeks and seeks and cannot find a door.

Only since the chemist's assistant had been living at
Wankas' could it happen that he sometimes had the feeling
of being at home. He liked to be in his little room and he
spent his free Sundays in front of the large desk, lost in the
heavy smoke clouds of his pipe, reading in old books, forgetting today and tomorrow over their yellowed pages. No
wonder he didn't hear a quiet knocking on his door, and
only sprang up in fright when Luisa entered and stood timid
and undecided behind the dense tobacco fumes. She was
like a dream in her faded, plain blue dress, with her great,
silent eyes, and because she carried flowers in her hand, three
small white roses, which seemed to nestle up to her shyly.

"Oh please, pardon me," she now said in German with
a slight Slavic intonation, "I thought you had already gone
out to eat . . . I just want . . . ," and now she walked past

him and stuck the three white roses behind a small portrait of Zdenko which hung on the outside wall. Land had often contemplated it. He saw now how her hands trembled with painful tenderness, and, completely absorbed in this gazing, he was unable to say or do or think anything. He heard the girl's voice once more: "His first birthday on which he is no longer with us" — and then everything was as before, he stood alone in the Sunday stillness of the chamber, and might now have gone on reading. Only he wasn't able to do so. He had to look again and again toward the door, as if expecting someone, and finally the smoke began to annoy him and he opened the window, so that the air of the clear February day streamed in fresh and bright. For a moment he felt very festive and thought, I have received noble guests: three white roses, and smiled as if in a dream.

In September many people come back to the city from their summers in the woods and from the seaside. They are no longer used to walking in the streets, and suddenly, before they know it, they're holding their hat in hand as in the woods, or singing quite loudly to themselves. This is because the memories have not yet gone to sleep within them. And when they meet one another, they are chatty and communicative. They feel how something like the luster of the last attenuated days rises up out of the narration and spreads itself comfortingly over the muggy streets and squares. Perhaps the two say to each other when taking their leave, "You're looking very well," and, "how you've changed." And they smile at one another for a moment, self-conscious and grateful.

So Luisa too had returned. Since early spring she had been away . . . There is a hot, hidden land. Glowing flowers behold themselves in black pools, while birds and clouds rustle above. White paths press between the trunks of tall, dark trees, discovering in these woods a noiseless, surging life. Figures appear in incomprehensible garments, and they may be people with sad expressions or with cool, smiling lips. At first it seems to you that you'd heard tell of them, and you have to recollect when and what it was. But they kiss you, and then you recognize in them friends whom you have loved and forgotten. And you want to kiss them again, regretfully. But their movements grow strange in the face of your salutation, and they fade back into the wide, waving woods, or else they attack you with gruesome, bleeding words and want you to give them your heart in exchange. It is a land of the young: children and youths, maidens and young mothers with their painful joy dance and feel their way along the shining countryside, their cheeks burning with a foreign felicity. But they don't see one another, for in their eyes there is no room for anything besides wonder. When they hear the other pilgrims lament or laugh, they listen and believe it to be the birds or the treetops or the breeze. They all have a single goal: the mountain of flames in the middle of the land. And from there many a one will not find his way home again.

But Luisa came back out of the land, which is called Fever, slowly and smilingly, through the groves of convalescence. Hesitatingly she recognized herself and her mother, who wept and kissed her hands, and the chamber, which was as if decked out with the golden, full light of September. It was a festive homecoming.

What days these were since her first outing! This ongoing reunion and greeting of everything and everybody. The people smiled, and the things shone so. She moved as if along a row of shimmering mirrors, which wanted to divulge to her how broad and tall she had become. She knew it, too. She felt strong and well rested. Without saying anything about it, she began to attend her lessons. She hadn't forgotten a thing, and even before Christmas she was able to give a little girl piano lessons herself. The little one had great respect for her teacher, yet in reality their roles were reversed. The love of this little being and its attachment called a crowd of new, joyful sensations to awaken in Luisa every day, and there was an attentiveness in her to which the child's questions sounded like lovely answers that bestowed a blessing. So much was happening to her all at once during these serene and uneventful days that she never found time to look out beyond yesterday; what lay behind seemed a single, great past and propitiation, out of which no shadow projected any longer into this new, rich life.

On Christmas Day Luisa entered the pharmacist's room.

"I just wanted to invite you, Mr. Land — please come and spend this evening with us, if you have no other plans."

Ernst Land smiled gratefully. Then he followed the girl's gaze and grew embarrassed. Over Zdenko's little portrait were three fresh white roses.

Luisa stretched out both her hands toward him: "You did that?"

"Always . . . ," and Land was annoyed at his blushes and quickly promised to come.

In the doorway the girl stopped again. "You are always so sad, Mr. Land."

Land said nothing.

"What are you thinking about?" and the look with which she asked this moved him so that he confessed with tears in his voice:

"About my mother."

On the evening of Christmas Day a strange, festive mood had come over these people. Even afterward it was reluctant to leave the rooms. It remained over everything like the quiet fragrance of pine, even when Mrs. Josephine, overcome by a sudden faintness, spent the long days in bed. Luisa quietly took all the little houshold duties off her hands, one after the other, so that she finally knew of nothing except this noiseless, darkening holiday behind half-drawn curtains, with the piping of the oven and the silvery chiming of the clock. In the evenings there were gentle, subdued conversations between the two women, and no yesterday appeared in them; only in the sound of the voices did it still quiver, in that of the mother as a quiet, timorous plea and in the words of the girl as a light, comforting forgiveness. And this was present still in the profound weeping with which Luisa one morning bent over her mother, who had gone from her without struggle and pain into a reconciled peace.

Just a week later Luisa took up her lessons once again. Her days were all filled to the brim with a crowd of pleasant duties, and although the nights broke in over her empty and anxious, she felt that even out of the darkness of sorrow no hostile dangers approached her any longer. In that stillness of her convalescence she had found herself for the first time, and had recognized herself so richly and far-reachingly that her most sacred self had not grown more lonesome through this loss. Grief only lay like a fine boundary on her smile and on her movements and could no longer limit the awakening of her spirit.

In February of this year there had still been a great deal of winter weather; only in March there came a holiday — it was the Feast of St. Joseph[23] — that made all the world merry. Not just that the snow still lay only here and there on hillocks and railway embankments, forgotten and despised — but a green had come over the liberated meadows, and overnight little yellow pussy willows rocked themselves to sleep on long, bare stalks in the mild, light-chasing wind.

Luisa had gone out to pray at the great noon mass in the Loretto Church. But then she had wandered, she could hardly say how, past the beckoning glockenspiel of the Capuchins[24] and had only looked up when she stood behind

23. March 19, a holiday that was enthusiastically celebrated in Austria.
24. The first Capuchin monastery in Bohemia was built in 1601 in Loretto Square on the Hradčany. Adjacent to it is the Loretto, a pilgrimage site constructed in 1626, which includes an exact copy of the Santa Casa in the Italian town of Loretto (allegedly the building in which the Annunciation took place). There is a famous glockenspiel at the Loretto shrine, built in 1694, which plays songs in praise of the Virgin every hour.

the Royal Garden in one of the broad, solitary avenues, her arms outspread. She sensed how much she loved everything around her, how much all this was a part of her, and that this quiet, joyful growth with its secret happiness and its sweet longing was her destiny, not that which people, in their dark craving, desired and erred.

On the way home the shining swarms of joyful people came toward her, and she paused with a smile and looked out over the bright, living landscape. One couldn't believe that all these laughing hordes would fit back into the narrow houses over there. This is because each of them has grown beyond himself into the shimmering day, which he barely feels on his shoulders. And the shining sky casts its golden luster so richly and rashly over the people and things that they forget to keep their everyday shadows and are themselves light in the glimmering land.

This image made Luisa think, she didn't know why, of Zdenko, and whether it ever happened to him during his shadowed life that people came toward him like this, luminous and happy.

Then she turned toward home. The shadows of the people lay grayly in the cold, abandoned streets, piled up like forgotten everyday clothes, and a dull winter smell seemed to emanate from them. Luisa shivered, and at the first, playful hint of the sloping sidewalks to run, she fell in merrily and just like a child she trotted downhill past the ancient palaces, the sulky giants at the gates staring down on her angrily. But she no longer feared them.

In the doorway stood Rosalka, relating, with many gestures, an important piece of news to the neighbor women who crowded around her, in which the women participated with eager nods. As soon as one of them had caught sight of Luisa, they all began to wave and call out in impatient confusion. A few children were screaming as well, and out of it all Luisa finally understood the single word "company." That sufficed to call forth the greatest astonishment. As she raced up the dark stairs, her thoughts were occupied only by a single, gigantic "Who?" With this curiosity in her eyes, she sprang into the room where Mrs. von Meering was waiting on the sofa with unconcealed annoyance, stiff and strict. But the greater amazement was really on the part of the colonel's wife, who had just now brought her condolences for the most recent misfortune and was in no position to display to this beaming, breathless child one of her elegant, kind words of mourning. She felt a powerful, righteous indignation toward this laughing healthiness, and felt herself just as superfluous as in that earlier case. "These people," she thought, "it must run in the family."

In the meantime Luisa had recovered enough for a few apologies, and she asked the lady politely about the reason for her visit. Mrs. von Meering hastily pressed her handkerchief in front of her face and sobbed out through a fold, "Your poor, poor mother."

When there came no response to this moving comment, the colonel's wife looked up and stressed with stern eyes, "She was a very respectable, good woman."

Luisa sat there with lowered gaze and contemplated — so it seemed — the toe of her delicate foot. The lady waited a while longer, and when Luisa still didn't begin to cry, she realized that all mildness and empathy would really be in vain with this obdurate girl. While her expression suggested that she was already beginning to get up, she added in a bitter tone of voice:

"I just wanted to tell you this one thing, my child. You must already have thought about the changes which have become necessary since the death of your good mother?"

"I don't know," Luisa stalled self-consciously.

"Of course, it goes without saying that you must immediately give notice to this young man, who, as I perceive with astonishment, is still living in your home."

"But —" Luisa let out with great, astonished eyes. Then a smile twitched across her face which was almost impish.

Mrs. von Meering was already at the door.

"I held it for my duty to make you aware of it. Of course, you may do as you please."

"Yes, ma'am," Luisa replied with sudden boldness and stood on her toes to reach the colonel's wife, who seemed to be growing larger and larger. Then she asked smilingly, "Wouldn't you like to rest a moment longer, ma'am?"

But the lady fled out of this dreadful house. She was already in the kitchen, where the old maid Rosalka threw herself toward her boisterously, to kiss the sleeve of the silk mantilla, with great reverence, somewhere near the elbow. The insulted woman tore herself away from this slavish worship with a curt "adieu," and found in the gaping of the housemates on the stairs and in the corridors, and in their whispering wonder, only a small compensation for this "mistreatment suffered."

Luisa stood there for a while, pensively. Rosalka had run forward to the window, to have another look at the aristocratic lady who, as she emphasized, was "at our place" for a visit.

When she came back again, she had very curious eyes.

Luisa didn't notice. She said while pacing back and forth, "I think we'll stay in this apartment. And I've completely forgotten to speak to you about that, Rosalka. You are in my service now, under the old conditions. You are willing, aren't you?"

The old woman swore to it on her temporal and eternal happiness, and in so doing it came about that she suddenly, in tears, addressed her mistress not, as she had from her childhood, as "Loisinka," but as "Miss."

Then Luisa knocked on Land's door.

He came toward her smiling. "You mole," she called to him jokingly, "always in your room. Today you must get out of the city for once. It's spring! I was far, far outside," and she made a gesture as if to show him where spring lies. Her eyes shone with such promise. Then she went on in an important, businesslike tone, "I don't want to bother you, Mr. Land. I only wanted to inform you of this. I am keeping the apartment; so everything continues as before — that is, if you are otherwise satisfied with the room?"

He sought her eyes and then quickly looked at the ground. "Oh," he said softly, "I like it very much here, I think . . ." He began to rub his palms together . . .

Luisa had kept her hand on the doorknob. "That's nice," she helped him and then was also somewhat at a loss.

He looked as if something were weighing on his heart.

The two young people were silent.

Then the girl began, "I would so like to learn German a bit better; perhaps you can use a little Bohemian in exchange."

"Yes," Land breathed with relief, "I love your language."

"So," Luisa offered happily, "then do, if you have time, come into the front room for a while. There are a few books there, German ones too."

And in the doorway she added: "Come as often as you like," and, more quietly, "you must tell me all about your mother."

A Bibliography of Related Works

Primary Sources

Rilke, Rainer Maria. *Nine Plays*. Trans. Klaus Phillips and John Locke. New York: Ungar, 1979.

——. *Sämtliche Werke*. Ed. Ernst Zinn, in association with the Rilke-Archiv and Ruth Sieber-Rilke, 6 vols. Frankfurt a.m.: Insel, 1955–1966.

——. *Zwei Prager Geschichten und Ein Prager Künstler*. Ed. Josef Mühlberger. Frankfurt a.m.: Insel, 1976.

Secondary Sources

Aschenbrenner, Viktor. "Rainer Maria Rilke — ein deutscher Dichter aus Böhmen." *Sudetenland* 18 (1976): 132–139.

Bethge, Hans. Review of *Zwei Prager Geschichten*. *Stimmen der Gegenwart: Monatschrift für moderne Literatur und Kritik* (February 1901): 79.

Černý, Václav. "Noch einmal und anders: Rilke und die Tschechen." Trans. Christian Tuschinsky. *Die Welt der Slaven* 22 (1977): 1–22.

——. *Rainer Maria Rilke, Prag, Böhmen und die Tschechen*. Trans. Jaromír Povejšil and Gitta Wolfová. Artia, 1966.

Cohen, Gary B. *The Politics of Ethnic Survival: Germans in Prague, 1861–1914*. Princeton, N.J.: Princeton Univ. Press, 1981.

Demetz, Peter. "The Czech Themes of R. M. Rilke." *German Life and Letters* 6 (1952–53): 35–49.

——. *René Rilkes Prager Jahre*. Düsseldorf: Eugen Diederichs, 1953.

Hofman, Alois. "Begegnungen mit Zeitgenossen: Hedda Sauers Erinnerungen an R. M. Rilke." *Philologica Pragensia* 9 (1966): 292–304.

——. "Das Heimaterlebnis René Maria Rilkes." In *Weltfreunde: Konferenz über die Prager deutsche Literatur,* ed. Eduard Goldstücker. Berlin: Luchterhand, 1967. Pp. 203–214.

Bibliography

Kisch, Egon Erwin. *Gesammelte Werke,* vol. 7, *Marktplatz der Sensationen.* 3rd ed. Berlin: Aufbau, 1967.

Kohlschmidt, Werner. "Prag — manieristisch gesehen: Beobachtungen zur Reimtechnik von Rilkes Gedichten aus der Prager Zeit." *Jahrbuch der Grillparzer-Gesellschaft* 12 (1976): 87–96.

Lorenz, Willy. "Rainer Maria Rilke und Böhmen." *Die Furche* (1947): 291–293.

Mágr, Clara. "Sprach Rilke tschechisch?" *Blätter der Rilke-Gesellschaft* 13 (1986): 83–92.

Mühlberger, Josef. "Das Herkommen R. M. Rilkes: Österreich, Böhmen und Prag im Leben und Werk des Dichters." *Sudetenland* 17 (1975): 241–255.

Naumann, Helmut. *Studien zu Rilkes frühem Werk.* Berlin: Schäuble, 1991.

Preisner, Rio. "Rilke in Böhmen: Kritische Prolegomena zum altneuen Thema." In *Rilke Heute: Beziehungen und Wirkungen,* ed. Ingeborg H. Solbrig and Joachim W. Storck. Frankfurt a.M.: Suhrkamp, 1975. Pp. 207–245.

Puckett, Hugh W. "Rilke's Beginnings." *Germanic Review* 8 (1933): 99–113.

Rothe, Daria A. "Rilke's Early Contacts with Czech and Jewish Prague." *Cross Currents: A Yearbook of Central European Culture* (1982): 255–266.

Rothmann, Kurt K. F. "Die Stilentwicklung in Rilkes dichterischer Prosa." Ph.D. diss., Univ. of Cincinnati, 1966.

Schwarz, Egon. *Poetry and Politics in the Works of Rainer Maria Rilke.* Trans. David E. Wellbery. New York: Ungar, 1981.

Seifert, Walter. *Das epische Werk Rainer Maria Rilkes.* Bonn: H. Bouvier, 1969.

Sieber, Carl. *René Rilke: Die Jugend Rainer Maria Rilkes.* Leipzig: Insel, 1936.

Stahl, August, and Reiner Marx. *Rilke-Kommentar zu den "Aufzeichnungen des Malte Laurids Brigge," zur erzählerischen Prosa, zu den essayistischen Schriften und zum dramatischen Werk.* München: Winkler, 1979.

Stephens, Anthony. "König Bohusch im Umkreis der frühen Prosa Rilkes." In *Rainer Maria Rilke und Österreich: Symposion im Rahmen des Internationalen Brucknerfestes '83 Linz,* ed. Joachim W. Storck. Linz: Linzer Veranstaltungsgesellschaft, 1986. Pp. 38–47.

Bibliography

Storck, Joachim W. "Rilke als Staatsbürger der Tschechoslowak-ischen Republik." *Blätter der Rilke-Gesellschaft* 13 (1986): 39–54.

Szász, Ferenc. "Zwischen den Kulturen. Kulturvermittelnde Ab-sichten des jungen Rilke." *Blätter der Rilke-Gesellschaft* 13 (1986): 29–37.

UNIVERSITY PRESS OF NEW ENGLAND
publishes books under its own imprint and is the
publisher for Brandeis University Press, Brown
University Press, University of Connecticut, Dartmouth
College, Middlebury College Press, University of New
Hampshire, University of Rhode Island, Tufts
University, University of Vermont, and Wesleyan
University Press.

Library of Congress Cataloging-in-Publication Data
Rilke, Rainer Maria, 1875–1926.
   [Zwei Prager Geschichten. English]
   Two stories of Prague / by Rainer Maria Rilke ; introduced and
translated by Angela Esterhammer.
      p.   cm.
   Includes bibliographical references.
   Contents: King Bohush — The siblings.
   ISBN 0-87451-661-7
   I. Esterhammer, Angela.   II. Title.
PT2635.I65Z4513   1994
833'.912 — dc20   93-35912
                                                              CIP